BROKEN SAGE

BROKEN PEAK PACK
BOOK 2

BY JULES CRISARE

BROKEN PEAK PACK

Broken Hero
Broken Sage
Broken Mage
Broken Rebel
Broken Crown
Broken Witch

HIDDEN RUNAWAYS

Hidden Trouble

BLACK HILLS VENDETTA

Wolf's Retribution
Wolf's Revenge
Wolf's Reckoning (*coming to Kickstarter in 2024*)

BOX SETS

Broken Peak Pack eBook Bundle Volume 1
Broken Peak Pack eBook Bundle Volume 2
Broken Peak Pack Omnibus Collector's Edition (*Kickstarter Exclusive*)

SILVER SENTINEL NOVELS

Destined Heir
The Last Immortal Mystery Files (*coming to Kickstarter in 2023*)

SENTINELS OF THE SILVER ORB

BROKEN SAGE

BROKEN PEAK PACK
BOOK 2

BY JULES CRISARE

SILVER ORB BOOKS

BROKEN SAGE

Designed by J. Crisare

0123pbk

ISBN: 978-1-948603-28-7 (pbk.)

To my fuzzy socks. They've kept my toes warm and are great fun when I feel the urge to slide across my hardwood floors (which I most definitely never do, because I'm a grown-up).

PROLOGUE

A History of Shifters & the Role of the McCallisters
—from Edna McCallister's journal

IN THE beginning, the Great Shifters took flight and ruled from the skies with the sharp talons of the Griffins and the Dragons' fiery breath.

So fearsome was their power, all creatures on Earth kept a healthy distance. Except one. A human female who didn't fear what was different and instead wanted to learn more about the Great Shifters. The Great Shifters tolerated her presence, and over time relied on her and her female descendants to keep their histories.

As the fated war approached, the great shifters planned accordingly. They sent the historian into hiding with the volumes of histories to secret away around the world. But before they sent their historian away, they instilled within her a drop of the magic living inside them.

Over time, the Great Shifters would turn from truth to legend, living in the imaginary worlds belonging to children, but a female descendant in each generation would be compelled to seek answers in the tomes of the past to keep the magic viable.

For in the future, when the Hero emerged, so too would a historian who would advise the Hero and become the Sage.

CHAPTER ONE

ELEANOR Ward ignored the vibrating cell phone as it bounced across the desk. Unrestricted access to the century and a half year old journal belonging to an Appalachian folk healer was limited and rare. She wouldn't allow the distraction of a phone call to shorten the brief time the librarian allotted her. Of the small number of grad students studying folklore at the University of Missouri, Eleanor was the only one working towards her Masters instead of a doctorate, but had been enrolled the longest. Officially, the school didn't have a part-time program for graduate studies, but the department head made an exception for her.

Her phone vibrated again. Either a bill collector or a telemarketer, and neither was more important than Eleanor's time with Edna Hern MacAllister's journals. Eleanor had given up her scheduled time last month. Foster experienced several days of uncontrolled shifting right in the middle of her scheduled time in the restricted area. The journals had to wait. Eleanor wouldn't risk Foster shifting at daycare in a room full of rambunctious three- and four-year-olds. But right now, she couldn't give up even five minutes or she'd never finish her thesis.

Foster usually experienced long breaks between shifts. At least six weeks, if not longer. Eleanor planned on taking advantage of the respite to make up for the lost research time. If luck became a close friend, she'd defend her thesis at the end of the fall semester, graduate in the spring with the others, and find a job that would help pay off her student loans and give her the freedom to keep Foster out of daycare.

Twenty-five more minutes with the journal, then she'd pick Foster up before heading home for a quiet evening. After he went to bed, she'd sit in front of her computer and put in a few hours of entering data from some random survey full of push questions that would never give the company the answers they needed all so she received a paycheck that would help pay the bills.

She could do it. She had the next three months planned out to the minute, but she could do it.

The phone vibrated again. Eleanor snatched it off the table and shoved it into the front pocket of her bag on the floor. Out of sight; out of mind.

She studied the entry on the fragile page she'd been reading before her phone interrupted her. The entry made no sense. Taking into consideration Edna's habit of spelling words phonetically and using local terms long extinct, the entry couldn't be accurate. According to Edna, the young man she had treated for a bullet wound healed in a few days. No one healed from a bullet wound in days. Not now with the marvels of modern medicine and not a hundred and fifty years ago in what was likely the most rural part of the United States.

Edna made a mistake with the days. She had to. But Edna didn't make mistakes. Edna was meticulous with the numbers in her notes. She recorded doses by weight and size, and times down to the second. The attention to detail was unusual, but especially so in the Appalachians. The entry had one other difference. Next to the patient's name, S. Roosevelt, Edna drew five small circles with a line coming out the top of each circle and one large circle underneath the smaller circles. Eleanor hadn't noticed any symbols on the entries before, but then she hadn't been looking for them.

After a quick glance at the wall clock, she flipped through the journal pages. This time she ignored the words and focused on finding doodles or drawings in the margins. For the first time in months, Eleanor felt as though she wasn't floundering with her thesis. She studied the role of magic in rural American traditions and folklore.

While Mr. Roosevelt's treatment didn't have any additional notes about spells cast, the speed of the recovery with the small symbol tickled at Eleanor's researcher senses.

"Eleanor!" Wayne Ritchie, her adviser, whispered yelled at her from the door of the private study room she occupied.

Eleanor jumped and the page in the journal ripped along the spine.

Shit. Shit shit shit shit shit. Eleanor didn't curse in front of Foster, instead she thought her swear words. If anytime was appropriate for swearing, it was when she destroyed a priceless and irreplaceable book.

"Eleanor." Wayne walked into the room, ignoring the torn page. "Why didn't you answer your phone? I've been calling."

"What? Why? Is there something wrong? Did I make a mistake about my scheduled time?" As she said the last word, Eleanor glanced at the torn page still in her hand and swallowed. The librarian would never allow Eleanor access to the journal again. She'd probably ban

Eleanor from the entire library too. With a deep breath, Eleanor filled her lungs with oxygen and willed her heart to stop racing.

"Come on. We don't have much time." Wayne lifted her messenger bag to the table. Though the bag overflowed with heavy books and caused Eleanor to tilt to the side when she carried it, he had no problem hoisting it up. He didn't speak while he shoved her papers into her bag.

"Wayne? Dr. Ritchie, what's wrong?"

Wayne lifted his gaze from the top of the table and gave her a small shake of his head. Eleanor had only seen the gesture in movies, the ones with an action hero intent on saving someone, but wanted them to stay quiet. Whatever worry she had about her academic standing fled and a worry a hundred times worse took its place.

Foster. Something must have happened with Foster.

Eleanor reached down and helped her adviser shove her notebooks and pens into the bag. Once Wayne and Eleanor packed up everything on the table, he slung the bag over his shoulder, grabbed her wrist, and tugged her out of the room. She stumbled behind him, doing her level best not to scream out her need to know what was happening.

Dr. Wayne Ritchie was unflappable. Four or five years ago, a student's water broke during the middle of his class. He calmed the student and found someone to take her to the hospital while he continued to deliver his lecture. If he was this close to a panic, it meant the worst-case scenario had happened. Her greatest fear had come to life.

Hurrying through the hallways, they bypassed the elevator and used the stairs. And instead of heading out the main doors, Wayne pushed open a side door that led to a small alley between two buildings.

Once outside in the fresh air, Eleanor opened her mouth. "What's going on?"

"Look, we don't have a lot of time. Save your questions until your son is in your arms and we're off campus."

Eleanor's stomach dropped. Not only was her worst fear materializing, somehow, against all reasoning, whatever happened was worse than she had imagined and planned for. Shit. All of her contingency plans included having enough time to do things like run to the bank and close out her checking account. Not that she had much money, but at least the balance wasn't negative. Once they got far enough out of town, she'd find a job waiting tables until she saved enough to make a real run for it.

She held no delusions that Foster's secret was still a secret. The only reason for her adviser to drag her from the library and say the words he just had was if Foster shifted in front of someone.

As soon as Wayne opened the back door to an older model SUV sitting at the end of the alley and Eleanor slid into the seat, the crying started. Fear and anger merged, feeding the tears sliding down her cheeks. Keeping Foster safe should have been her priority. This was all her fault. If she hadn't tried to finish her degree and put Foster in daycare when she had classes, none of this would have happened.

She worked from home so she didn't need to put Foster in regular daycare. In another year, she planned on filling out the forms for homeschooling. But she convinced herself a few hours a week would be okay, and Foster would benefit from the socialization with kids his own age. The excuses didn't absolve her of the sin of putting her education ahead of Foster's security. It wasn't like Foster's life was all that spectacular to begin with, and Eleanor made it worse with one selfish decision.

Wayne got in the passenger side of the front seat. Eleanor didn't recognize the man behind the steering wheel. He looked similar enough to Wayne to be his brother, and her mind categorized him as a friend. Since Foster came home with her, she learned how to assess and categorize strangers. Eleanor brushed the back of her hands against her cheeks, erasing the tears, but not the red blotches on her cheeks. She couldn't hide the blotches with a tub full of expensive makeup way out of her budget once Foster entered her life.

The driver pulled into traffic with the slow caution of someone learning to drive. It didn't take long to drive across campus, but they took the back roads and avoided the heavier traffic. By the time Eleanor's brain processed everything that had happened in the last ten minutes, they were pulling up in front of the daycare center and there wasn't time for her to ask questions.

Wayne turned in the seat and offered a reassuring smile. "Go inside and pick up Foster, Eleanor, then come right back out. Everything will be fine, we just need to get him out of there as soon as possible. Keep things normal, okay?"

"Yeah. Normal. Okay." Eleanor nodded. She could do this. She'd done it before. This wasn't a new task she'd never attempted before. Except once her feet hit the cement walkway, it was impossible to stop her feet from hurrying. She needed to see Foster. She had to keep him safe. No matter what happened or would happen, keeping Foster safe needed to be her only concern.

Not knowing what to expect, relief washed through her when she didn't find police officers swarming the building. Maybe the worst didn't happen. As soon as she opened the door, Foster threw himself at her and wrapped his arms around her knees. Eleanor looked over at the teacher as she bent down and hugged Foster close to her.

"How you doing, little man?" Eleanor combed her fingers through his blond hair. Foster looked nothing like his mother, and Eleanor figured he must have gotten his hair, and possibly other things, from his father.

"Good. Ms. Sara helped me today." Foster struggled with the R sound the way so many children did and replaced it with a W sound.

"She did? That was nice of her." Eleanor glanced back at the front door, remembering Wayne's advice to leave as soon as possible.

"Where's your coat and backpack? In your cubby? Why don't you go grab them, then we can pick up a pizza for dinner."

It was only the afternoon, but she didn't have any other excuse to hurry Foster out of the building. As Foster raced down the short hallway to the cubbies, Sara approached Eleanor. With nowhere to run, Eleanor practiced several lies in her head. She didn't know what happened, but just because it wasn't the worst didn't mean it wasn't bad.

Sara reached out and squeezed Eleanor's shoulder. "There was an incident today. It will be okay, but you need to accept the help being offered, Eleanor. You can't do it alone, no matter what you think."

Eleanor gaped at Sara. What did the teacher know about Eleanor's needs? Sara kept her lips together when she smiled, but the hint of a sharp and long tooth peeked out before Sara's blue eyes did the same glowy thing that Foster's did. And it wasn't caused by the light hitting them and reflecting back in an odd way. Sara's eyes had the full-on glowing like the ass end of a lightning bug thing happening.

"Incid–"

Sara did the slight head shake, the same gesture Wayne made in the library. Eleanor snapped her mouth closed. Wayne's appearance at the library made a little more sense. Maybe. If she closed one eye and twisted her head to the side and pretended everything that happened since bringing Foster home was normal. She still didn't understand what was happening or why, but at least she wasn't alone. Well, Foster wasn't alone. Others, like him, existed.

"Hurry scurry, little mouse." Sara called down the hallway and the sound of Foster's pounding feet against the linoleum immediately followed. Sara smiled at Eleanor and gave her a quick one-armed hug. "It will be okay. Now hurry up or Wayne will worry."

Eleanor reached for Foster with one hand and his backpack with the other. Before heading outside and into an unknown future, Eleanor mouthed the words thank you to the young teacher. Eleanor had a feeling Sara kept Foster safe today and prevented the worst thing from happening.

"Who's Wayne?" Foster tilted his head back, so he looked at Eleanor when he asked his question.

"Dr. Ritchie. He gave me a ride today." Eleanor wanted to say more, but the teacher was already walking down the hall to the classroom.

"Oh. I know him. Why did he give you a ride?" Foster's questions never ended once they started.

"He just did. Wasn't that nice of him? Come on, let's go." Without Sara in the hallway with her, Eleanor no longer felt safe and wanted to leave the building and get back into the SUV as soon as possible.

As they walked out of the building, Eleanor's mind reeled with all the new information assaulting her. It hadn't been more than thirty minutes since Wayne grabbed her and her life had changed even more than it had the night she became a mother. When she suddenly had the heavy weight of the responsibility of a newborn resting on her too small shoulders.

Wayne got out of the SUV and greeted Foster with a fist bump. "Let's get you in the car and buckled up."

Eleanor hadn't even thought about a car seat, but someone had. It hadn't been in the back seat when she got out, but there it was now. Foster crawled up into the SUV and then into the seat, insisting he could do it on his own the entire time. He turned four in a few weeks and his independence streak was a mile wide. It always had been. When he took his first steps, he refused any help from Eleanor and relied on the furniture instead. When Foster turned two, he announced to Eleanor it was time to stop wearing diapers and potty trained himself.

Wayne looked over at Eleanor and gave a slight head tilt toward the front seat. "Why don't you sit up front with Victor?"

Well, that was unexpected. Wayne checked that Foster was secure, then hurried around the back of the SUV instead of crawling across the car seat. Eleanor got into the front seat. Again, Victor pulled into traffic with all the caution of a new driver. He also went exactly one mile over the speed limit and used his turn signals even in the right turn lane where no one used them.

The low rumble of a man speaking quietly came from the backseat, but Eleanor couldn't make out the words. When Foster's high-pitched voice responded, she could only make out a few words, but it seemed they were just talking about what Foster learned in school.

Victor glanced over at Eleanor before returning his gaze to the road. "Who's the father?"

Eleanor closed her eyes and let out a long breath. She didn't hide the fact that Foster was technically her nephew and not her son. But then she didn't make a point of telling everyone either. Foster saw her as his mother and anytime someone learned of his parentage, it always caused weird conversations that left Foster confused. When he was older, she'd explain it to him, but it was too much for a three-year-old, even one who was a few weeks away from turning four. "I don't know. And neither does his biological mother. Why?"

"Because you can't do this alone. We have someone who can help if you don't have an idea who the father is, but you can't stay here."

Eleanor looked over her shoulder, but Foster wasn't paying any attention to her. Wayne captured all of Foster's attention.

"What happened today?" Eleanor asked the question she'd been wanting the answer to since Wayne interrupted her research.

"He shifted. Sara and two kids witnessed it, but no other adults. We don't know how it's going to play out with the kids, but you can't stay here. Taking Foster to his father would be best, but since you say you don't know who he is—"

"I don't."

"Fine. The father is unknown, so that leaves you with a last resort."

In Eleanor's experience, last resorts never ended well. She'd accept the help temporarily, but she was going to find Foster's father and get the answers she needed.

CHAPTER TWO

WAYNE handed Eleanor the keys to the SUV, a pay-as-you-go cell phone, and a printed map with directions to an isolated area just outside of the town of War, West Virginia. "The phone isn't smart, you have to go old-school. If something happens, and you take longer than two days to get to War, call Mac or he'll send out a search party. In fact, plan on calling him when you stop tonight and tell him where you are."

Eleanor stared at the set of keys resting in her palm. Everything happened so fast and without any hiccups. From picking up Eleanor at the library to sending her out of town, it ran like a well-oiled machine. "Have you done this before?"

"No, but we had a plan in place in case something like this happened. We aren't fools, the secret will get out. But in the meantime, we do what we can to keep the damage to a minimum." Wayne set a heavy yellow envelope on top of the keys. "This will help. It's not enough for you to start over on your own, but it will get you to where you need to go and then some."

"You don't–"

"I'm not," Wayne cut her off. "We've gotten good at hiding things in plain sight and will take care of the rest of your things."

"But what about my landlord? He's going to wonder where I ran off to when he doesn't get the rent check on the first of the month."

"No, he won't. Like I told you, we're good at making things go away."

Eleanor bit down on her bottom lip and looked away from Wayne's steady stare. She had so much to say to him, but had no idea where to start. Wayne took pity on her and gave her a one-armed hug. Slightly awkward, but he was just her academic adviser a few hours ago. Now, he was her savior.

"You'll want to get on the road soon if you want to get to War before Friday. And I need your phone. Part of making you disappear is convincing whoever's looking for you that you're somewhere else entirely."

"Okay," she prepared for this.

When Victor and Wayne explained lots of shifters lived in the world, Eleanor realized what a risk she and Foster were to their secret. They knew about Foster because she arrived at her interview for grad school with Foster because she didn't trust anyone enough to leave him alone with when he was an infant.

After they told her where she was going, Eleanor excused herself to go to the bathroom. Once she closed and locked the door behind her, she called her sister. Bethany spent the first five minutes denying she remembered the name of Foster's father. Eleanor finally offered Bethany money for the name. Thank God for apps and Western Union. Minutes after making the offer, Bethany received a notification that she had 200 dollars waiting for her. Two-hundred dollars Eleanor couldn't afford if she had to drive twelve hours across a third of the country, but she'd go without if it meant she'd finally have the name. If Eleanor had any hope that her sister wasn't a horrible person, it went away as soon as Bethany said the name *after* she received the money. Nice to have confirmation that Bethany gave Foster up when he was born because it was best for her and not what was best for him.

Four years ago, Eleanor had no plans of being a mother. Her focus was on finishing school and finding a grad school program while keeping as far away from her mother and sister as possible. Then the hospital called and informed Eleanor that not only was she listed as her sister's emergency contact, but her sister was in labor. Eleanor's biggest worry shifted from how she was going to pay off her student loans to how she was going to afford formula and whether store brand diapers were as good as the name brand versions.

Three months after bringing Foster home from the hospital, his first shift happened. Shifting from human to wolf wasn't something you called the pediatrician about, not unless you wanted to see your son nabbed by some government organization and poked and prodded. Or worse. And reasoning with a three-month-old baby was impossible. Keeping Foster's secret became her priority until he was old enough to understand secrets and why some secrets were more important to keep than others.

Eleanor handed her phone to Wayne. "I owe you and your brother a lot."

"You'll do fine, Eleanor. And once you're settled with Mac, we'll figure out a way for you to complete your degree. If nothing comes about with the two boys who saw Foster partially shift before Sara intervened, I'll work something out with the department head."

"And if the parents believe their story?" That was the reason Eleanor wasn't hiding with Wayne and Victor. If the story leaked and made its way to the media, Eleanor and Foster needed to be far away from Columbia.

"Then we'll figure something else out. Now get in the car and drive." Wayne kept his arm around Eleanor's shoulder and guided her to the driver's side door. "The sooner you get to Mac, the better."

Eleanor's fingers tightened around the steering wheel as she sat in the parked SUV in the middle of the Walmart parking lot.

The clock on her phone read 4:36 pm. The GPS told her she would reach her destination in sixty-three minutes.

Numbers and notifications that didn't offer up the answer Eleanor needed. Was she doing the right thing?

Jackson.

No last name, or maybe Jackson was his last name. Eleanor didn't know.

She should have told Wayne she found the name of Foster's father. Wayne might have helped her find him instead of sending her to West Virginia. But what if Jackson tried to take Foster away from her? Eleanor was Foster's mom. She'd been there through the teething, the first words, the first steps, and the first shift. If Jackson took Foster from her, she wouldn't be able to fight it without putting Foster at risk of becoming a science experiment for the government.

Jackson, whoever he was, was a risk she wouldn't take. Mac might be a stranger, but she trusted Wayne and Wayne trusted Mac. That would have to be enough.

"Mommy?"

"Yeah, baby?" Eleanor pried her fingers from the steering wheel and turned in the front seat so she could look at the little boy whose fingers and face were coated with a healthy dose of orange dust.

"Want one?" Foster held up the small bag of cheese puffs she bought for him at the last gas station they stopped at.

She hadn't expected the giant Walmart so close to their destination and didn't want to risk a bathroom break at a place where the sound of dueling banjos wouldn't be out of place. When Foster found the Cheetos, she couldn't say no. He'd been so well-behaved and hadn't complained once during the drive. Plus, he only asked if they were there yet every few hours instead of every few minutes.

The cash Wayne had given her wouldn't last long if Mac couldn't or wouldn't help them. Expecting the worst-case scenario, Eleanor tried to stretch the money by not stopping at fast-food chains for meals and sleeping at rest areas instead of a hotel.

If Mac sent them away and everything went wrong, the cash in the envelope was her safety net and she didn't want to waste it.

Eleanor was sixty-three minutes away from finding the answers she desperately needed, or sixty-three minutes away from the worst defeat in her entire life.

They could stay the night in the Walmart parking lot and head out in the morning to save herself from having to drive back in the dark and possibly lose out on the ideal parking space far away from routine traffic and smack dab in the middle of two lights. Except what difference was two hours (and probably a quarter tank of gas) now or tomorrow?

If she had to come back to the Walmart parking lot to sleep for the night, she'd also be walking into the store in the morning to see about a job. And maybe a super cheap motel with a super kind and generous old lady who would take care of Foster for her while she worked a below minimum wage job. Admittedly, the last two possibilities straight up belonged in a movie or book and had no business dancing through her mind. Yeah, Eleanor's life sucked at the moment. But it didn't suck as much as it would have had she stayed in Columbia, and Wayne hadn't been there to help.

"Mommy?" Foster's tiny voice reminded her she hadn't answered his question.

"No, baby, but thank you."

"Are we almost there?"

Foster had trouble with his Rs, so his words came out more like *awe we almost thewe.* The speech impediment stumped most adults who spent little time with children, but Eleanor was adept at deciphering the chatter of an almost four-year-old.

"Hmm? We're about an hour away." Eleanor responded without thinking. If her thoughts hadn't wandered off into worst-case-scenario land, she would have come up with a non-answer answer. Now, she couldn't be a coward and spend the night at the Walmart parking lot. She couldn't tell him plans had changed, and they were going to do some car camping in a parking lot. He was fast losing interest in the novelty of car camping.

Eleanor bounced her head against the headrest and closed her eyes. How had her life come to this?

The weight of everything that happened settled on her in a heavy lump of near despair. She couldn't cry in front of Foster, and it wasn't like she could escape to the bathroom for an ugly cry in private.

Self-doubt be damned. She had to do what was best for Foster. And who knew? Maybe a super nice old lady lived with Mac and would watch Foster for a few minutes while Eleanor had an ugly cry in private.

One thing she was sure of though, Foster was hers and she would do whatever it took to keep him safe.

Eleanor released the emergency brake of the old Ford Explorer and shifted it into first gear. Her knee was going to hate her after this trip. The highway driving was no problem, but the hills and pot-hole ridden roads she encountered once she entered the Appalachians held a vendetta against both the SUV and her knee.

"Are you ready to roll, Foster?"

"Yeah!" Foster raised his chubby arms over his head and clapped his little hands together. "W!"

"Yep, that's a W." For all Eleanor knew, he was identifying the M.

When Foster was awake during the drive east, he had pointed out the letters he found on the signs along the highway. Eleanor fell into the habit of agreeing with his observations without confirming the actual letter shape. For all she knew, Foster's idea of the alphabet was completely different from the Latin one taught by most kindergarten teachers. But his preschool teachers hadn't mentioned any letter problems.

"Mommy?"

"Yeah, baby?"

"How much longer?"

Eleanor would have banged her head against the steering wheel if she hadn't been concentrating on avoiding the cavernous pot holes threatening to swallow the Explorer whole. "A while, baby."

"How many more minutes?"

"See this number right here?" Eleanor tapped at the clock on the car radio.

"Yeah?"

"When the numbers say five four five, we'll be close." Glancing in the rear-view mirror, she smiled at Foster leaning out the left side of his car seat to better see the clock. "Why don't you read me one of your books?"

Foster didn't read, but his imagination was great when it came to describing the pictures on the pages of his books. Lately, Foster's stories centered on wolves, and it didn't matter if a wolf was pictured or not.

She focused on the last miles of her drive while Foster's voice filled in for a radio that only picked up NPR.

The potholes were so aggressive that Eleanor wondered if they were sentient and moved across the road to trap unwary drivers. Navigating the obstacles of the road combined with the concentration required to time her shifting between second and third gear to handle the hills passed the time faster than she expected.

Or maybe time flew by because she feared what awaited her and Foster once they got outside of War and into the even more rural neighborhoods. The temptation to roll down the windows and listen for dueling banjos was almost too great.

The voice on the GPS demanded Eleanor turn left, except it wasn't onto a road. Or at least not a road by most people's definition since it came to an abrupt halt before a wall of trees. The GPS voice chided her to continue driving, but Eleanor didn't think the SUV would win an arboreal battle. She shifted into neutral and yanked up on the parking brake, chasing after a rolling car once was a lesson not easily forgotten. They would have to walk in the rest of the way.

"Ready for an adventure, baby?" Eleanor unfastened her seatbelt and looked over her shoulder.

"Yeah!" Foster emphasized his excitement at finally being there with a vigorous wave of his arms high above his head.

"Put your books in your backpack while I get out to open your door." Eleanor stood next to the driver's side door and stared out into the woods while letting out a long breath and looking down at the map "What did you get yourself into, Eleanor?"

Not that she expected an answer. Too many unknowns and a whole lot of guessing got Eleanor nowhere.

Time to cowboy up.

She pulled her wallet from her purse before dropping it in the trunk with the rest of their bags. Eleanor didn't know what to expect, but she knew trekking through the woods with an almost four-year-old in tow was enough additional baggage. By the time she reached Foster's door, he was unbuckled from his car seat and had his orange dusted fingers and face pressed against the window.

"Let's go, little man." Eleanor opened the door for him, and Foster exploded from the backseat in a ball of barely contained energy. "Don't race off, there could be wild animals in the woods."

Or scary moonshiners. But Eleanor didn't say those words aloud.

Foster skidded to a stop and looked up at Eleanor with bright green eyes on the cusp of glowing. A tiny growl rumbled from his chest as he pulled his eyebrows together. "Don't worry. I'll protect you, Mommy."

His declaration tore at the strings of her heart. "I know you will, baby. But I want to protect you too."

"Okay. We'll protect each other." He skipped across the gravel-covered ground back to her, stopped to slip his backpack over his small shoulders, then wrapped his arms around her legs.

Sure, she might now be covered in orange dust from the waist down, but the slight gesture comforted her. Eleanor ruffled his hair and smiled down at the top of his head. "Okay, baby. I just need to grab a bag and then we'll go. You have everything you want to bring. We can come back and get something, but probably not until tomorrow morning."

Eleanor looked up at the sky. It would be dark soon, and even if Mac couldn't help them, he might feel enough sympathy to let them stay the night. Or so she hoped.

"Yep. My books. My toothbrush. My cars. My crayons." Foster continued listing the contents of his backpack, but stayed close enough for her to keep an eye on him in her peripheral view.

Eleanor dumped out the bag she used for books and repacked it with a few changes of clothing she bought from a discount store they stopped at as soon as they crossed over the Missouri border. Edna's journal caught her gaze. The worn leather cover reminded her of the symbol that had triggered the idea of Edna hiding something in her entries. Foster, breaking into the baby shark song as he skipped around the SUV waiting for her, reminded Eleanor that her research would have to wait. She pushed the journal and the desire to look more closely at the pages away.

"Okay, little man, let's get ready to roll." Eleanor rested her hand on the top of the rear door, ready to slam it down. At the last minute, she snatched the journal from the pile of books and shoved it into her bag between a pair of jeans and a long-sleeved t-shirt embellished with a pink crown over the chest. Not her first choice, but they left their clothes behind and her wardrobe choices were at the whim of the bargain bin. The rear door slammed into place and Eleanor double checked the Explorer was locked up. She didn't know how safe it was to leave the SUV in the middle of nowhere, but wasn't sure where else to park it.

Foster skidded to a stop next to her and reached up for her hand. "Ready! And don't worry, Mommy, I keep you safe and you keep me safe. Right?"

For Foster's sake, she wished it was as simple as protecting each other. She squeezed his hand. "Right, baby."

CHAPTER THREE

A NEW scent drifted through the air, but Jackson couldn't identify it.

The others in his pack hadn't noticed it. Or maybe they had. But Finley and Tevin weren't about to interrupt their impromptu wrestling match because Tevin caught Finley drinking from a mug that Finley had signed his name on. It didn't matter that Tevin signed the mug ten years ago. The young wolf believed the mug to be his. Allard found more fun in egging on the fighting males than playing peacemaker. And Leighton was loath to stop any of his lessons with Vixen, their new Alpha female, to intervene.

Jackson stared into the tree line, as though he could see through the massive trunks and thick branches and discover who the scent belonged to.

Bray, the Alpha male of their small pack and Vixen's mate, stepped next to Jackson and crossed his arms over his chest. "What do you know?"

"I thought..." Jackson hesitated. There had to be a right answer or Bray wouldn't have asked him, but he was damned if he knew what it was.

"I didn't ask what you think." The grizzled Alpha narrowed his eyes as he looked off into the distance.

"Someone is in our territory."

"That's too broad, Jackson." Vixen barely looked away from her sparring. "Give specifics."

"What?"

"Wait?"

Both Finley and Tevin stopped their wrestling to look up at Bray and Jackson. Even Allard seemed more curious about Jackson's observations than maintaining a running commentary on the wrestling match.

Bray rolled his eyes and ignored the others. "Start with feelings."

"Something's off."

"Okay. Now, go through your senses. Which one caused you to notice?"

"The scent."

"What scent?" Finley pressed the side of Tevin's face into the ground while swiveling his head around to look at the tree line.

Tevin's muffled reply came at the same time. "There's no outsider scent."

"Good. Focus on that." Bray continued ignoring the others.

Bray's attention unnerved Jackson. He wasn't used to his Alpha guiding him along. Ever since Bray claimed Vixen as his mate, he had picked up some of her ways. More teaching and less commanding. Advice from Vixen was great. Guidance from Bray scared the hell out of Jackson. Mostly because he figured he'd get it all wrong.

"It's unfamiliar, but somehow still belongs."

Bray's head snapped to Vixen, who stepped away from Leighton and stared at Bray. Flipping the dagger she'd been practicing with around in her palm, she slid it into the holster and strode across the lawn to stand in front of Jackson. Her head cocked to the side, and she studied him with an odd gesture resembling both a raptor and a feline.

"Can you tell what it is?"

"Wolf." Jackson responded without thought.

"If the scent belongs, how can it be a wolf and unfamiliar?" She wasn't asking to trick him.

"I don't know. I haven't scented it before, but it…"

"It belongs." Bray finished for him.

"You feel it too?" Jackson asked.

"No. But then I didn't identify a scent. My wolf just let me know something was off."

"Same with my voice."

Vixen's voice belonged to the scariest beast any of them had ever seen. Through some legend that Jackson didn't understand, or really care about, a griffin lived inside Vixen until Bray freed it with a claiming bite. Oh, and the griffin could speak too. And fly. And rip out a man's spine.

But Vixen's griffin and Bray's wolf only knowing something wasn't right in their territory didn't answer why Jackson identified the scent as unfamiliar but belonging.

Vixen exhaled a long sigh and stared up at the darkening sky. "Well, do we send out a search party? Or wait for them to get closer?"

When Bray didn't answer, Jackson realized she was asking him. "Um…"

Vixen looked out the corner of her eye at him and grinned. "Well?"

"Wait."

Vixen and Bray shared one of their looks. Once Vixen's animal appeared, they had this weird silent communication thing going on. It freaked Jackson the hell out. Especially when he figured out they held entire conversations with each other without saying a word.

"Good enough." Vixen clapped her hands three times and looked over at Tevin and Finley. "Oi, you two. Stop your rough-housing and start dinner. Leighton, why don't you and Allard patrol the river from the waterfall to the base of Mount Baldy. I doubt it's a distraction, but better to be safe than sorry."

As the four other wolves wandered off to complete the tasks Vixen set them on, she stepped closer to Bray. He wrapped his arm around her shoulder and pulled her against his side.

Not that Jackson ever expected to find a mate, but if he did, he hoped she was like Vixen. Capable, but understanding of the protectiveness of dominant males. He might not have been thrilled when Vixen first arrived. Especially when she brought him to his knees, and not in the good way, when she was half injured.

Jackson, Bray, and Vixen stood in a line, shoulder to shoulder, watching the tree line.

Waiting.

CHAPTER FOUR

"FOSTER?"

"Yeah, Mommy?" The little boy looked up from inside the valley of a steep ravine.

"How d'you get down there?" What Eleanor wanted to ask was how in the hell he climbed the near vertical three foot dirt wall without breaking his neck, but opted for the less anxiety-ridden question.

Foster stretched out his arm and pointed to a path impossible to find if you didn't already know about it.

"How did you..." Eleanor shook her head and brushed away the thought with a wave of her hand. He wouldn't be able to answer the question any better than he had every other time she asked how he always seemed to know where to go and how to get there.

She didn't want to consider the how or why of Foster's newfound orienteering abilities. Ever since they left the SUV, Foster had been scampering through the woods as though he lived here his entire life. She grabbed hold of a sturdy enough looking branch and half skidded, half slid down the side of the embankment. How they would climb up the other side was something she'd worry about later.

They'd been walking through the forest for almost thirty minutes and hadn't seen any signs of civilization. In the next few minutes, Eleanor would have to decide whether to give up and turn back or press on. Foster wouldn't last much longer. He'd already exceeded all of her expectations. Fifteen minutes into a walk in Columbia and Foster begged for a piggy back ride. Not to mention, getting lost in an unknown forest where mean moonshiners might live wasn't top on the list of smart plans of action.

Eleanor reached down and took Foster's hand in her own. She looked up at the three foot climb they were about to attempt. Three feet shouldn't be too difficult. She could push Foster up and hope he stayed put while she hoisted herself up. "Ready for a boost, buddy?"

Foster giggled. "Noooo!"

"No? Why no?"

Foster pointed to another trail leading up from the valley. This one was as hidden as the other and this time Eleanor couldn't ignore the fact that no one should know about them unless they lived in the area.

Curiosity overcame her desire to remain ignorant that this was more than a little boy who turned into a wolf because of some weird accident of genetics. "How did you find these trails, Foster?"

He lifted his shoulders in an exaggerated approximation of a shrug he'd seen a cartoon character do on TV. Great. Eleanor didn't expect a short and concise answer, but she hoped Foster would have given her something more than the body gesture equivalency of no clue.

As it turned out, Foster required a boost to clear the top six inches. And Eleanor relied on the assistance of a few branches and modified curses muttered under her breath. The branches helped more than the g-rated swear words coming out of her mouth, but grumbling criminy and sugar and fudge sauce made her feel better about the physical reminder of the stupidity of the plan Wayne and Victor came up with.

Foster stood at the edge of the shallow ravine and peered down at her. "You're doing good, Mommy."

She wasn't. And she was pretty sure Foster knew she wasn't either since he used a similar tone of voice she used when encouraging him during his attempts at something new. As she pulled her weight up over the final bit which required more arm strength than she believed she had, Eleanor flopped on her back and stared up at the darkening sky through the heavy branches. "Give Mommy three minutes, buddy, then we'll go."

Foster crouched down next to her head and stared at her. He bent forward and lowered his head, providing her with a cinematic close-up of his eyes. His eyes did that glowy thing again before he pulled his head up and fell back on his bottom.

Eleanor held the map to her face and studied the highlighted yellow path that was supposed to take them to Mac. According to the map's scale, her finger, and her best guess at their location, they were ten minutes away from their destination.

Impossible.

When she got out the car, she was sure it would take at least an hour walking. With Foster, she figured it would be closer to an hour and a half. It wasn't possible, no matter how she looked at the map, to cut the traveling time in half.

She'd worry about the possibility of impossibilities after she found Mac and learned how he was going to be the solution to all her problems. "Okay, buddy, I think we're ten minutes away. Ready to go?"

Foster jumped to his feet and pumped his fists in the air. "Yes!"

Eleanor attempted a sit up. And failed. She tried again. And once more, she failed. Foster grabbed her hands, dug his little heels into the ground, and, with the aid of her non-existent stomach muscles, helped pull her to her feet.

Hand-in-hand they continued through the trees, which seemed to not be as thick as they had been before the mini ravine. Each step brought them closer to her goal and added to the growing list of doubts.

Foster tugged on Eleanor's hand. "Mommy? Who are we visiting? This isn't where Aunt Bethany lives."

Eleanor swallowed back the urge to come up with a small fib. One of the many she used when talking about Bethany. She hadn't lied to Foster. He knew Eleanor adopted him and Bethany was the woman who gave birth to him, but she tried to protect Foster from Bethany's complete lack of interest in him. Hence using the term aunt, that and it didn't add layers of a complexity the teachers at Foster's school had no interest in explaining to his classmates.

"We're visiting someone Dr. Ritchie knows. A friend of his and Victor's."

"Does he know we're coming?"

"Hmm?"

Foster stopped and if Eleanor didn't want to drag him along behind her, she had to stop too. He raised his arm, like some scary little kid in a horror movie, and pointed straight in front of him.

Her gaze followed his arm to his finger and the old man standing a few feet away from them. "Holy double hockey sticks."

Everything about the old man fit her wildest imagination of what a moonshiner looked like. Except he didn't have a gun. Eleanor figured any moonshiner or booze runner would carry a shotgun at least.

A long beard covered the bottom portion of the old man's face and wrinkles traversed the skin she could see. He pulled off a dirty hat, revealing a wild field of thick gray hair. "You must be Eleanor and Foster. I'm Mac. And this here, is Roose."

A man so enormous he would have dwarfed the offensive line of an NFL team, stepped out from behind the old man. He gave her a polite nod and a small smile in greeting, "Eleanor."

How the hell had she not seen them. Or heard them. She grabbed Foster by the back of his shirt and pulled him in behind her, but he scrambled around to stand in front of her legs. She smiled. What else could she do?

"Are you friends with Dr. Ritchie? He's nice. He told me he's my friend. So that makes us friends."

Eleanor covered Foster's mouth with her hand before he could ask any more questions or share any more information.

The old man, Mac, chuckled and stuck the hat back on his head. "Come on then. Let's get you someplace warm."

"Uh, Mac?" Roose stepped next to Mac and Eleanor took a step back.

Roose might be a gentle giant, but he was huge. Like bigger than Fezzik huge. Thinking about *The Princess Bride* reminded her she needed to find a copy of the book. Foster and she had been reading it before bed, but like so many of their other belongings, it got left behind.

Mac brushed Roose's question away with the wave of a hand. "I know. When Wayne phoned, I suspected, but yeah. I know. It throws a little wrench into our plans, don't it?"

Roose grumbled. Or maybe he growled. Regardless, the noise was enough for Eleanor to take another step back, keeping Foster as close to her as possible.

The sound of dueling banjos danced through her thoughts. Mocking every wishful idea she had come up with during her drive across the country.

This was such a bad idea.

Maybe, if she picked up Foster and backed into the woods, they'd let her leave unmolested. Before she could implement her plan for a great escape, which was arguably only a smidge less stupid than the plan to drive halfway across the country, Foster pulled away from her and ran towards the two men. Right towards the one who looked as though he knocked down trees by punching his fists into the trunks.

"Foster! No!" But it was too late.

Foster stopped in front of the giant man, who was a hundred times larger than she originally thought, and zoomed around him in tight circles.

"Cute kid." Roose, who also had a beard (magnificent by most standards but nothing close to the catastrophe living on Mac's face), watched Foster circle around him for a few seconds before looking up. His dark brown eyes settled on Eleanor. "But he's not yours."

Roose didn't ask a question. He made a statement. One that didn't leave any room for argument according to his tone.

Yeah. This was bad on so many different levels. When someone commented about how Foster looked nothing like Eleanor, she passed it off with a smile and politely explained he was adopted. For whatever reason, the adopted word stopped any more questions from being asked. But then no one who commented knew the secret Eleanor had been keeping about Foster. Mac knew about the secret and she assumed Roose, whoever he was to Mac, did too.

"He's mine." She hated the idea of biology counting for more than everything she and Foster had gone through together. "In all ways that matter, he's mine."

Roose cocked his head to the side and sniffed the air. "Except for a big one, right? Presumably the reason you're here in the middle of nowhere, wondering what the hell you've gotten yourself into."

"Let's get some food in your belly, boy, and answer the questions nagging at your mom." Mac ignored the standoff between Eleanor and Roose and snagged Foster by the back of his shirt, pulling him from his current lap around Roose. "And then we'll just rip the band-aid off, 'cause there's no other way to ease into this mess."

"Mess?" Eleanor asked before she could stop the words from leaving her mouth, but Mac was already heading away from them with Foster in hand.

The giant looked up at the sky and exhaled long and loud. "These the only bags you have?"

The question shook Eleanor back to reality. "What? Yeah, no."

"Well, which is it?" Frustration lingered on the edge of his words.

"I left some things in the car."

Roose held his hand out, "give me the keys, I'll get the rest of your things. And best to move your car too."

Eleanor hesitated. If she handed over the keys, it would be impossible to run. But she couldn't leave Foster alone with a stranger and she couldn't demand he come back to the SUV with her and Roose. Of all the options available, not one was even halfway close to good.

"Eleanor?" A soothing rumble replaced the frustration in Roose's voice. "This isn't a good situation, I get that. But the way I see it, for Wayne to call Mac, he exhausted the other options. You don't have to trust me or Mac, but you trust Wayne or you wouldn't have gotten in that car with your little boy and driven here. Wayne trusts Mac. Hell, I don't think there's any of us who doesn't trust that old codger. He's crazy as shit, but he's a good male."

She reached into her pocket and pulled out the keys. The speech wasn't going to lead a platoon into a victory against all odds, but it eased the anxiety building up since the moment she shifted the old SUV into gear and pulled onto the highway. Roose was right. She placed her trust in Wayne and it had gotten her this far. Now she needed to place her trust in the men Wayne placed his trust.

Eleanor handed over the keys. "It's by th–"

"I know where you parked. Just like we know when you pulled up. Now hurry up after them, before Mac gives your boy some of his real coffee, as he likes to call it. He doesn't differentiate much between kids and adults since everyone is younger than him by a lot." Roose closed his hand around the keys and slipped off into the woods.

Before she lost sight of Mac and Foster, she trotted after them, hoping she wouldn't trip over any of the roots or branches criss-crossing the path.

CHAPTER FIVE

WHATEVER hopes Eleanor had of finding a haven with Mac fled as soon as they walked into the small cottage. Unless Mac's house held some magic and belonged in a fairytale, there was no way Eleanor and Foster could stay there. The house didn't even have a bedroom, just a bed pushed into a corner and a small kitchen off the main room. A single closed door along the far wall either led to the bathroom (she hoped) or the backyard and an outhouse (she figured was more likely).

"I'd say make yourselves at home, but since we're gonna tear the band-aid right off, I'll say make yourselves comfortable for the time being instead." Mac buried his head in an old refrigerator that should have been retired and stuck in a trash heap twenty years ago.

Eleanor took a deep breath and plastered a smile across her face before she looked down at Foster, who had done as Mac suggested and was making himself comfortable on a large couch covered with one of those crocheted afghans.

"Hey, Foster, why don't you pull out a book to read to Mac and me while I fix you something to eat." At least she had the sense to pack the bread and peanut butter in her bag.

"What book?"

"Your choice." Eleanor pulled out the sandwich fixings and brought them to the kitchen while Foster started telling them all about green eggs and ham, the favorite meal of a wolf named Sam.

"What in nine hells is that?" Mac glared at the food in Eleanor's hands.

"Well, our dinner, but specifically, peanut butter and some bread."

"I know *what* it is, I meant what's it doing in my kitchen?"

Eleanor refused to allow herself to be ashamed. It wasn't a great dinner, but it was food, and her son wasn't going hungry eating a basic sandwich found in most pre-schoolers' lunch bags. "I'm making Foster a sandwich."

"Not with that you aren't." Mac pulled a large roast from the fridge and dumped it on the counter. "Make him a sandwich with that."

"That? What is that?"

"Beef. The boy is growing and peanut butter isn't helping him." He pulled a large carving knife from a drawer and set it next to the roast.

Mac wasn't wrong and Eleanor put her pride aside, pretty much what she'd been doing since Wayne pulled her from the library, to make Foster a sandwich with food that didn't come from a jar.

Mac wandered into the room with Foster and sat down next to him on the couch. She watched the two of them with their heads bent together. For the first time since getting in the car and driving, Eleanor had a moment to herself. Mac looked over his shoulder at her and winked before turning his attention back to Foster, who had glommed on to the old man as though Foster had spent his entire life with him.

Eleanor wiped the back of her hand across her cheek. Stupid tears. She hadn't cried once during the drive. She had wanted to, but didn't dare in front of Foster. And now, in a strange place, with strange people, the tears came despite all her efforts to keep them at bay. She turned away from Foster and Mac and focused on cutting the meat for Foster's sandwich. With her back to them, the tears had the freedom to fall without being seen. With luck, Foster wouldn't notice her blotchy cheeks if Mac and the sandwich distracted him.

She took extra time arranging the thick slices of meat on the bread and cutting the sandwich in half on the diagonal, hoping those seconds would give her cheeks time to turn from red to pink. Once satisfied with the sandwich, she grabbed a paper towel for Foster to use as a plate and carried the sandwich out to them.

"Oh," she handed the sandwich to Foster, whose eyes bugged out at the sight of the large sandwich, "I should have asked, did you want one. Mac?"

"Nope. We have a few minutes yet if my calculations are right." Mac slid the book from Foster's lap and shook his head. He pointed the book in the general direction of the closed door. "Why don't you do that freshing up thing women do. And yes, I have running water and a toilet that flushes."

Eleanor looked down at Foster. It was one thing to be a few feet away from him in another area of a one room building, but it was another to be in a room separated by a closed door.

"Go on, lass. Not sure when you'll get another chance."

Mac talked in riddles. She had no idea what he meant and didn't want to ask in front of Foster. That was probably his plan. She used the same tactic before and would use it again. Adults censored their words in the presence of children. Mac must have spent enough time around children to understand that and to use it to his advantage. She reminded herself that Wayne trusted Mac, and she trusted Wayne. In the world of math, they called that the transitive property.

"Are you sure?"

"I'm sure. Now go before the boy finishes his sandwich and you lose your chance."

Eleanor shoved her doubt aside and escaped to the bathroom. It wasn't as bad as she expected. The small shower and bathtub took up half the room, the toilet flushed, and everything was clean. The worst part about the small room was the mirror above the sink that revealed just how tired she looked.

One quick sponge bath with hot water later, Eleanor looked like a different person. Too bad she didn't feel like one.

"Oi, Mac, what's so important that it can't wait for the morning!" A woman called out from outside the cottage.

Eleanor tripped over herself to get out of the bathroom and in front of Foster before the stranger came inside the cottage. She barely trusted Mac because of Wayne, and that trust tangentially included Roose, but Roose was as far as the transitive property reached. She found Mac watching the door with his head cocked to the side and Foster peering around Mac's shoulder.

"Oh. Well, this is unexpected." The woman stood in the open doorway staring at Foster. She tilted her head forward to get a better look "Yeah, I can see how waiting wasn't an option."

Roose pushed the woman inside and tossed the car keys to Eleanor. "Your car is in a safe spot and I got your bags."

A "Vixen, this here is Eleanor. And the boy is Foster. Foster and Eleanor, this is Vixen. A friend." Mac leaned back on his couch and grinned. "I expect the others will be along in a few seconds."

If Eleanor went by appearances alone, she'd have grabbed Foster and locked the two of them in the bathroom. Mac might have called

Vixen a friend, but the woman had a scary calculating look to her. The only thing keeping Eleanor in place was that Vixen hadn't taken more than a few steps into the room.

Vixen shook her head from side to side and narrowed her eyes at Mac. "I hope you didn't arrange this for entertainment purposes."

Eleanor grinned. Whoever this Vixen was, she had no problem calling out Mac. And from the red flush on Mac's ears, her accusation wasn't off the mark.

"Brace yourself. Things are about to get even more wild." Vixen stepped to the side and pulled Roose with her, leaving the doorway open.

The conversation left Eleanor confused. She didn't understand what anyone was talking about and still didn't understand why Wayne sent her to Mac or how he could help them.

"Damn it, Mac. Vi and I were about to have a nice evening together. This better be good." A dark haired older man, somewhere in his early forties, stepped into the small cottage and came to an abrupt halt as soon as his gaze landed on Foster, "oh."

"That's what I said, Bray," Vixen reached for the man's hand and pulled him to her.

Eleanor stepped closer to the back of the couch and rested her hand on Foster's shoulder.

"Jackson, you're going to want to step inside for a moment." Bray called through the open door.

Jackson?

It couldn't be. What were the chances? Maybe Jackson was a common name for shifters. Eleanor did her best to convince herself that the man Bray called to wasn't the same Jackson her sister named. And it was working too. Her mind rambled through the list of reasons it was impossible. Well, at least until the man walked through the doorway.

Jackson, she assumed, wasn't as big as Roose but close enough for Eleanor to have to tilt her head back to look at his face, had the same color hair as Foster. The same eyes. The same chin and jaw. His forehead even crinkled the same way when he concentrated. At least Eleanor assumed Jackson was concentrating from the way he stared at Foster.

Eleanor stepped around the couch, plopped down on the cushions, and pulled Foster into her lap. She wrapped her arms around him and pulled him tight against her body.

Jackson's mouth dropped. He stepped back until his body pressed against the wall. Eleanor recognized the shock. She'd experienced it several times over since Foster came into her life.

"Mac?" Jackson's voice shook. Whether from fear or anger, Eleanor didn't know.

Foster looked at the three unknown faces and smiled. "Are you friends with Doctor Ritchie? I am too. So that makes us friends."

"That's one way to put it." Vixen smiled, but kept her gaze on Jackson.

Jackson stood still and silent. The only movement came from his blinking eyes and the opening and closing of his mouth. As though he wanted to say something, but couldn't form the words.

Foster squirmed in an attempt to wriggle free, but Eleanor was prepared for the move and tightened her arms.

Mac cleared his throat and stood. "Wayne called me. Asked if I could help a friend out. Seems there was a bit of a kerfluffle back in Missouri and Foster and his mom need a place to stay for a while."

"Mac," Jackson's voice still shook, but this time Eleanor knew it was from anger.

"Your questions can wait, Jackson." Mac trampled over Jackson's words. "Now, Eleanor needs a place to stay. Roose and I don't have much in the way of extra space and our friend Gareth has a spare room, but he's probably not the best candidate."

Bray rolled his eyes, Roose snorted, Jackson fumed, and Eleanor leaned back into the far corner of the couch keeping Foster close to her. Mac chuckled. Or it might have been a cough. Eleanor couldn't tell.

Of everyone present in the room, Vixen was the calmest, as though she spent her life dealing with one crisis after another and this one ranked low on her panic meter. Eleanor envied her.

"Mommy, you're holding me too tight." Foster announced to the room and bounced on her lap.

"Mommy?" Jackson, Bray, and Vixen asked at the same time.

"Like I said. You all can wait. I think there are other things we should talk about first." Mac looked down at Foster. "Want to take a walk? Get some of that energy out of you? We can head over to Bray and Vixen's place, since that's where you'll be staying."

"They are?" Once more Jackson, Bray, and Vixen spoke at the same time.

"We are?" Eleanor chorused a few seconds behind them.

For the second time in her life, a shifter took over Eleanor's life. At least she assumed Mac and the others were shifters. Why else would Wayne send her to them?

CHAPTER SIX

FOSTER wove between the legs of the adults as he raced along the path to the pack's Lodge. Every leaf and squirrel and rabbit and blade of grass needed to be examined and then shown to his mom. His excitement was understandable. The kid smelled like fur. And not just any fur. The kid smelled like a wolf.

Foster was a miniature version of Jackson. Even down to the way his forehead crinkled when he concentrated on something and pulled his eyebrows together. Luckily for Jackson, he had plenty of opportunities to see that particular expression, because Foster had it every time he found something to show Eleanor. He was the quintessential wolf pup. Curious as all shit and fearless. Foster's wolf had to sense the animals lurking inside the other grownups, but it didn't stop the boy from announcing his friendship with all of them.

Jackson let out a long breath and slowed his pace, lagging further behind the others. His gaze strayed from Foster to Eleanor. Jackson liked that name. Eleanor. It was old-fashioned, but somehow it fit her.

She looked nothing like the kid. Eleanor's hair was so black, it was almost blue and her eyes were such a deep dark brown, they could have been mistaken for black. But she had freckles across her nose and cheeks. The woman was the walking embodiment of Snow White. And a far cry from the blond hair and blue eyes of Foster. In fact, the only thing the woman and boy had in common was the freckles.

But Jackson couldn't scent any fur on the woman. She was all human. Jackson had slept with human women before, but he didn't recognize Eleanor and he was positive that if he *had* spent a night with her, he would have remembered. Besides, human women didn't have shifter children.

None of it made any sense. Not Foster, not Eleanor, and not their sudden arrival.

Foster broke free from Eleanor's grasp and barreled right into the back of Bray's knees.

Bray grumbled out a growl. The kid stopped running, balled his tiny hands into fists, and stared up at Bray with huge eyes. Foster tucked his trembling bottom lip between his teeth, but it didn't stop his chin from quivering.

Oh, shit. Jackson recognized that look. The kid was gonna cry. Tevin used to try it on Bray when he was younger. It never worked on Bray, but then Tevin wasn't as young as the kid.

"I'm sorry." The kid's voice trembled as much as his bottom lip and his R's turned into W's making the way he spoke really fucking cute.

"Foster, come back here." Eleanor snagged Foster by the sleeve of his shirt with a picture of the Hulk emblazoned across the front and pulled him back into the protective shelter of her body. With a defiant lift of her chin and a gleam in her eye, she faced down Bray with a look that promised harm to anyone who dared threaten the boy.

Vixen, who had been leading the group, stopped when Bray's growl rumbled through the woods. She turned and cocked her head to the side in that odd way that warned the wolves in her pack that her griffin was pushing her way to the surface. They had all learned firsthand how fierce the griffin was, but she was also curious. The problem was the griffin was like an overgrown puppy on steroids in some respects. She didn't know her own size or strength and could hurt someone without meaning to.

Jackson's wolf came forward from his sulking and studied Vixen, studying Foster. Both man and wolf prepared to jump in front of the kid and Eleanor if Vixen got a little too curious.

Foster mimicked Vixen, but leaned his head back to meet her gaze. Eleanor stepped back and pulled the boy with her. Jackson and his wolf shared the same thought. Smart woman.

Vixen crouched down, bending her knees to the side and placing her fingertips on the ground.

Crap. If her griffin came out, then all hell would break loose. Even Bray, who had sort of relaxed since Vixen's arrival, was his pre-Vixen tense self.

Vixen kept her gaze on the boy and smiled. "Do you know what we have at the Broken Peak Lodge, Foster?"

"That's me!" Foster shouted out in a high-pitched voice that filled Jackson's wolf with curiosity.

"Yes, you're Foster. And guess what's waiting for you at the lodge? A giant yard filled with leaves and grass and toads and turtles. And once we get there, you can run around the yard until you don't want to run around anymore. But we need to get there first. So how about you hold on to your mom's hand until we get closer to the Lodge?"

Foster narrowed his eyes and pulled his little eyebrows together before nodding his head with the enthusiasm of a bobble head toy. "For as long as I want?"

Vixen nodded.

"Okay."

Well, that was unexpected. Jackson's wolf settled back on his haunches, relaxing and the others in their group all exhaled a relieved breath before continuing on their way to the Lodge.

Bray slowed and fell in next to Jackson. "How long are you going to avoid the others and not say anything?"

"Until I figure things out."

"You haven't learned from the months Vi's been here that figuring things out on your own never ends well?"

"Have you?"

"I'm not the one who's just now realizing he's a father and has been for a few years."

"I don't recall you ever talking to any of us about Vixen and deciding to claim her as your mate. And we aren't even sure he's mine."

"Jackson, I had both Mac and Roose to help me figure things out with Vi. Since I don't think either of them will be much help in this situation, that leaves either me or Vi."

"Maybe I want to talk to Leighton or Allard."

Bray threw his head back and laughed. Jackson would have laughed too if Bray's questions hadn't annoyed him.

When the laughter ended, Bray put his hand on Jackson's arm and stopped them. "The way I see it, Foster is going to stay with us or we'll find a pack willing to take him. If the kid's wolf is anything like yours, he won't last in a pack for long. And finding one willing to take the woman too? That'll be a long shot."

"You'd let a human stay here? With Broken Peak Pack?"

"You think I'd be okay with separating a mom from her kid?" Bray smacked Jackson's shoulder with the back of his hand. Hard.

Jackson rubbed his shoulder. "But she's human."

"Yeah, somehow I don't think Vi would be happy if I used that as a reason to separate Eleanor from Foster. Besides, I didn't know about Vi's griffin before I decided I wanted her to stay."

"Vixen wasn't human. We didn't know she was a shifter or that a fucking griffin was hiding inside her, but we knew she wasn't human. Plus Vixen is strong as shit and can take down all of us at once without breaking a sweat," Jackson grumbled.

"Yes she can." Bray grinned and stared at Vixen's back as she moved further away from them. "So, assuming finding a pack for Foster and Eleanor isn't an option, you going to be okay with her staying here?"

Jackson rolled his eyes. Leave it to Bray to ask the question without easing into it. "Why wouldn't I be?"

"Because you just learned you're a dad. I imagine that doesn't settle too well with you, or anyone really." Bray scratched his fingernails across the beard stubble on his cheek. "If I put a pup in Vi, and she left, then came back four years later, I think I'd be pissed."

"But that's just it. I didn't put a pup in Eleanor. She's not Foster's mom. At least not the one who gave birth to him. I'd remember her. If I slept with Eleanor, I'd remember her, but I don't. And she's human."

"You don't remember her at all?" Bray ignored the human portion of the argument.

"Bray, hand to God. I have no fucking clue who she is. Until Roose came and dragged us to Mac's, I didn't even know I had a kid."

Bray lifted a shoulder in an approximation of a shrug. "Maybe he's your half-brother."

This time Jackson snorted. Bray's statement didn't need a response.

Foster was Jackson's son. That still left the mystery of who Eleanor was to Foster and the question of what she would be to Jackson.

"Why are you sure you'd remember her?"

"Because I'd recognize her scent. With that dark hair and fair skin, she's like a hot grown-up version of Snow White. And her eyes are beautiful with those lashes. I'd remember her."

Bray raised an eyebrow and leveled his stare at Jackson.

"Her freckles are sexy too. I didn't think freckles could be sexy, but on her they are."

"You don't say." Bray smirked.

The asshole found Jackson's predicament funny.

Jackson clamped his mouth shut and glared at the trees behind Bray.

Bray slapped Jackson's shoulder. "You have a pup, Jackson. You're a dad and you have a pup and that pup comes with a mom who is human."

Instead of the disappointment or anger Jackson expected to hear in Bray's voice, he sounded almost gleeful. Well, as much as any response from the Alpha could be called gleeful.

Bray not being upset should have been a good thing. Having the support of his Alpha should have put Jackson at ease. Except the opposite happened. The weight of Bray's words crashed down on Jackson's shoulders and chest.

Jackson was a dad.

A dad.

Jackson had a kid.

A kid who also had a mom.

A human mom.

His stomach dropped to his knees, and he swayed on his feet. Jackson would have gone over if Bray hadn't caught him.

"Bend over. Put your head between your knees. And don't forget to breathe."

"Brayyy." Jackson squeezed his eyes closed. Maybe the world would stop spinning and his stomach would return to the right location.

"It's not bad yet. Just wait until the kid tries to call Vi grandma." Bray didn't hide his amusement. At least he kept a hand on Jackson's elbow, stopping him from falling over.

Jackson took a deep breath before a full-blown case of hyperventilation took over. "What if she leaves and takes the kid with her?"

"She showed up here because someone pointed her in Mac's direction. I don't think she has anywhere else to go, Jackson. Eleanor leaving here with the kid is the last thing she wants. It might be what she expects though. And if Vi's taught me anything, it's that you won't be able to make the decision for her. Eleanor has to come around to staying on her own. Unless you want her to leave?"

"My wolf wants the kid to stay. If she comes with him, then so be it." Jackson grumbled out, his voice muffled since his head was still between his legs.

"Keep telling yourself that, Jackson."

Jackson groused, still bent in half. "When did you turn into the wise old man?"

"You really need to ask that?" Bray slapped Jackson on the back and hurried down the path to catch up with the others.

No. Jackson didn't need to ask the question. Bray's wisdom arrived around the same time he claimed Vixen. Somehow Jackson didn't think Foster would bring wisdom for him.

Another wave of doubt washed through him. Except this time Bray wasn't there to catch him. Jackson was going to make a horrible father. His legs buckled, and he went to his knees.

On the brighter side, things couldn't possibly get worse.

CHAPTER SEVEN

ELEANOR stopped in front of the large house built into the side of what most people would consider a mountain and stared. No wonder Mac decided Eleanor and Foster should stay here instead of his small cottage. The lodge, as the others called it, was closer to a mansion. It was something she expected to find in a mountain resort and not in the outskirts of a town in the heart of the Appalachians.

"Mommy!" Foster pulled down on Eleanor's hand and danced from foot to foot. "I have to peeeee!"

"Well, let's go inside then. Foster can use the bathroom in my room and then we can get you settled in your own rooms and see what they have cooking in the kitchen for dinner." Vixen suggested as she came up from behind and Eleanor went along with it.

Vixen swept Eleanor through the front door, past a large living room, and down a hallway to a door that led to a bedroom. Foster broke free from her hand and charged into the room.

"Foster wait." Eleanor reached to stop him, but he was too fast.

"The kid's gotta go. Don't worry, we've all been there at some point. Just through that closed door next to the window, Foster." Vixen chuckled as Foster raced to the bathroom with dancing steps. As though that would prevent any accidents.

Without being too obvious, Eleanor glanced around the bedroom. She couldn't identify anything personal, but something told her she was standing in Vixen's bedroom. Besides the large bed and the usual dresser and small tables by the head of the bed, two large chairs sat in front of the large window that looked out over the yard. For being off the beaten path, literally, the house bordered on luxurious.

"You don't know us and I'm willing to bet hearing Mac inform you that you'll be staying with us instead of him is frightening. But I'm guessing that the reason you ended up here is the same reason Mac thinks you should stay here." Vixen sat down on a chair and stretched out her legs in front of her. The regal elegance she displayed came without effort and Eleanor wondered how Vixen learned that casual authority. "When I first came here, I didn't know anyone either. I doubt our reasons for being here are even remotely similar, but I will make the same promise to you that Bray made to me, Eleanor. As long as you are here, both you and Foster are safe. No harm will come to you. I promise."

Before Eleanor could process Vixen's words or promise, a plaintive cry came from the bathroom. "Mommmmmy! I need help."

Grateful for the distraction, Eleanor opened the bathroom door, halfway expecting to find a mess. Instead, Foster stood in the middle of the bathroom, his Ironman underwear hoisted higher on his waist than absolutely necessary, and his jeans tangled around his ankles.

"Foster, I told you, you don't have to take your pants off when you go to the bathroom." Eleanor closed her eyes and shook her head at the sight. The battle of whether pants remained on Foster when he went to the bathroom had been a long running one. Foster insisted removing his pants was an imperative with such conviction that Eleanor wondered if he'd keep up the habit when he was an adult.

Vixen snorted from her perch on the chair. Though the open bathroom door hid her, Eleanor imagined Vixen shared a similar perplexed look. Raising a boy had taught Eleanor the unexpected should not only be expected, but planned for.

"All right then." Eleanor stepped into the bathroom and knelt in front of Foster before he toppled over. "Put your hands on my shoulders. That's it."

Foster had twisted his jeans around so one leg was inside out and the other right side out. He had created a Mobius strip with his jeans and hadn't even had to remove his shoes. Slippers thwarted her loose fitting pajama pants, how tennis shoes conquered the restrictive fabric of denim confounded her.

"Ow, Mommy." Foster jerked his foot away as she wrangled the twisted pant leg free of his ankle.

"Well, if you didn't take your pants off, your jeans wouldn't be twisted, would they?"

Foster's eyes widened in shock and his jaw dropped in disbelief that Eleanor dared to question the necessity of removing his pants. She knew better than to question his bathroom ritual, especially in a bathroom, but the sight of the shower and the toilet with a lid, something she hadn't seen since leaving Columbia, distracted her.

"Mommy," Foster chastised her audacity, "you know I *have* to."

Eleanor rolled her eyes and bit down on the tip of her tongue. She loved Foster with everything she had, but he could also frustrate her. His need to remove his pants resided at the top of the frustrating items list. She got his pants back on then snapped and zipped them up, despite Foster's insistence he could do that on his own.

"Okay, all set. Now, wash your hands, please."

The simple task of applying soap to wet hands and rubbing them under running water before rinsing the soap off and drying with a towel became an adventure for a three-year-old fast approaching his fourth birthday. The stream of water needed minor adjustments to meet with his strict expectations. Foster also had to examine the counter while rubbing the bar of soap across his palms in slow motion.

A quick glance around the bathroom revealed nothing breakable and Eleanor left Foster to his own devices. Hurrying up hygiene always came back to bite her in the backside later. When she returned to the bedroom, Vixen's gaze locked on Eleanor and something about Vixen's eyes lifted away the lingering unease.

"When Foster's done, we can send him to the kitchen. I'm sure Bray and the others can handle finding him something to eat and drink. Then we can talk or maybe you'd rather have a few minutes alone? Or a shower?"

As nice as a hot shower sounded, leaving Foster alone with near strangers, even if one of the near strangers was probably Foster's father, rattled Eleanor's nerves. What if something happened and Foster changed into a wolf?

Foster charged out of the bathroom and skidded to a halt in front of Eleanor. He raised his arms up over his head and waved his clean hands in the air, waiting for an inspection. His appearance saved Eleanor from answering.

"Foster?" Vixen leaned forward over her knees and smiled at both Eleanor and Foster.

His head snapped around and he studied the woman much the same way she had studied him outside.

"Can I see the great job you did cleaning your hands?" Foster didn't hesitate. He raced over to Vixen and held his hands out, offering an unrestricted view of his palms and even between his fingers. Vixen reached for his hands and held them in her palms. "What an outstanding job. I might have you give lessons to some of the boys who live here."

Foster's little chest puffed out at the compliment. "My mommy taught me. She could teach them too."

Eleanor stared down at the top of Foster's head and smiled. Her little boy protected her in ways she never expected.

"See this hand here?" Vixen lifted Foster's right hand. "Well, if you go out to the hall and turn towards this hand, you'll get to the kitchen. Bray is there. You remember Bray, right? The big guy with dark hair?"

Foster nodded. "The pushy man?"

"Pushy?" Eleanor questioned. None of the men had made a physical move against either Eleanor or Foster. The last word she would have used to describe Bray was pushy.

Foster freed a hand from Vixen and rubbed his chest. "Yeah, pushy. He pushed here."

Eleanor's eyes widened and for several seconds she considered grabbing Foster and running back to the SUV. Except she had no clue where Roose parked it.

"Eleanor, I promise you. No harm will come to Foster or you while you are here. I swear." Vixen repeated her earlier promise.

Foster's smile grew until it took over his entire face. "I know."

Eleanor shook her head and bit down at the bottom of her lip. How did Foster know? And why was her barely four-year-old son making that announcement? Vixen glanced at Eleanor over the top of Foster's head. All would be revealed later. Or maybe Eleanor was reading what she wanted in Vixen's facial expressions. And what kind of name was Vixen, anyway?

"Yeah, so Bray is in the kitchen and I bet he has something good to eat and some juice too. Why don't you find him? Remember, when you leave the room, turn to this hand." Vixen lifted Foster's right hand. "Then follow the hallway to the kitchen. And make sure Jackson sits with you, okay?"

Foster gave Vixen a solemn nod then turned and skipped out the room. "Bye Mommy."

"Wrong hand." Vixen called out as Foster turned left instead of right.

Foster circled around and charged down the hallway toward what Vixen claimed was the kitchen.

"Children are special. Even the most impatient of us will tolerate a multitude of annoyances if a child is the cause." Vixen looked up at Eleanor and gave her an understanding smile. "So. Shower first or conversation first?"

Eleanor bit down on the tip of her thumb. Vixen's words didn't ease her doubts. It was the tone of her voice. "Conversation."

Vixen bent her head to the empty chair across from her. "In this case, I think it's best for you to start."

Eleanor sat down, but when she opened her mouth to speak, no words came out.

Where to begin? Her son changed into a wolf? Eleanor had a feeling that wasn't Vixen's reason for their little talk. The most likely reason for Vixen separating Eleanor from the others was the blond behemoth of a man who was the grown-up version of Foster. But that would mean having to explain why Eleanor hadn't told Wayne she learned the name of Foster's father and why she didn't share it with Mac at the first opportunity.

Vixen encouraged Eleanor after several minutes of silence. "I won't promise to keep all of your secrets because there are others who live here and I need to keep them safe as well. I will promise to only share what I need to and only with Bray. But for now, you don't have to worry about anyone else hearing your story."

"It's a long story."

"I gathered, hence the offer of the shower first. But ripping the band-aid off is less painful than pulling it away slowly." Vixen leaned back in her chair and stretched her legs out in front of her. "Jackson is in the kitchen. Bray, and now Foster, will keep him from sneaking back up here to eavesdrop."

"What? Why would I worry about Jackson?" Eleanor didn't even believe her protest.

"Because there's a miniature version of Jackson heading to the kitchen as we speak." Vixen pretended Eleanor's question was genuine instead of an unsuccessful attempt at deflection. "That you didn't recognize him as soon as he walked through Mac's door hints that the story is more complicated than any of us think. So why don't you start from the beginning. And when you want to take a break, tell me."

Eleanor leaned back in her chair and stared out the window. The problem with having someone addressing all of her concerns meant that telling her tale was all she was left with. Like Vixen said, she started at the beginning.

"First, Foster is my son, but through adoption. My sister Bethany is his biological mother."

Vixen's forehead furrowed, but she didn't interrupt Eleanor's story. And that established the pattern. As Eleanor explained how she took on the role of mother and did her best to raise Foster, Vixen's face expressed her frustration at the situation. But at least Vixen didn't ask any questions. Not until the end, when Eleanor admitted Bethany gave her the name Jackson but Eleanor kept that information from the men helping her.

"So, why are you here? From your story, you and Foster were doing just fine on your own. Why'd you give all that up to come half way across the country?"

Eleanor swallowed hard. Yeah, she delivered the sanitized version of her story. The one that didn't include her son sprouting fur and fangs and claws in front of a few classmates. She took a deep breath, closed her eyes, and let the words spill from her mouth. "My son turns into a wolf and he didn't get it from his mother. We did our best to keep it a secret, but we might have exposed what Foster is."

When Vixen didn't call Eleanor crazy or demand Eleanor and Foster leave because everyone living in the house was at risk, Eleanor opened one eye.

Vixen sat back in her chair with half a smile on her lips. "You didn't come here looking for Jackson?"

Eleanor opened her other eye and shook her head. "No. Until the day I left, I never had a name, and I didn't even think Wayne's friend would know Jackson much less live close to him.

"I should probably explain why Mac wants you to stay here. He'd want you to stay here even if Jackson wasn't living here. Mac isn't a wolf. And I'm guessing Wayne isn't one either. Wolf shifters are very similar to their wild counterparts and they do best in packs while the other shifters are fine on their own. In Foster's case, I imagine a young pup will do much better in a pack setting where he can learn manners and how to be a wolf from other wolves."

"Mac isn't a wolf?"

"Nope. But it's rude to share another shifter's animal, and it's impolite to ask. So until Mac shows you his animal or tells you, I need to respect that tradition."

Eleanor leaned back in the chair. Vixen's refusal to share Mac's secret was reassuring.

"I need to know something though. And keep in mind your answer won't change anything. You said Foster's secret was exposed but we haven't heard anything in the news. Is that something we should be worried about?"

Eleanor shook her head. "I don't think so, but I don't know. Wayne said it was only Foster's classmates who saw something, and it wasn't like he shifted into a wolf."

"What about your sister?"

"I don't think she has any idea. I had to pay her for Jackson's name."

Vixen nodded once, satisfid with Eleanor's answers. She smiled and her voice softened. "So, I suppose the next thing to decide is whether you trust us enough to go take that shower you've been doing your best not to look at while we talked, or head down to the kitchen so you can see with your own eyes that Foster is safe before you take your shower."

"Maybe we could..." Eleanor didn't know how much time had passed, but it felt like hours. She trusted Vixen, as much as she could trust a complete stranger. There was something about the woman's demeanor and voice that lulled Eleanor into a sense of safety. Something she hadn't felt since Foster shifted for the first time. But she wanted to see her son. She needed a final bit of reassurance before she allowed herself the freedom of a few minutes of solitude.

Vixen pushed herself out of her chair and reached a hand out to Eleanor. "You don't have to say it. Let's go check that Foster is still breathing before you lock yourself in the bathroom for as long as you need."

CHAPTER EIGHT

JACKSON leaned forward, resting his elbows on the table as he watched the kid next to him stare at the smorgasbord of food Bray and the others had set out. Cookies, chips, bread, meat, cheese, apples, bananas, hell, even Tevin, who only offered to help when Vixen witnessed it, had volunteered to cook up some macaroni and cheese. If it was in a cabinet or the fridge and edible, it found its way onto the table.

"How about a grilled cheese?" Bray asked after Foster hadn't reached for any of the food. "With ham or turkey or some roast beef?"

The kid nodded. But then the kid nodded at everything, which was how the pile of food had ended up on the table to begin with. He even nodded at the blue cheese stuffed olives. Vixen would kill all of them if her stash got raided by a kid who couldn't even appreciate the delicacy. Not that anyone else in the pack appreciated the olives. Stinky cheese in the middle of brined fruit that no one had any business eating wasn't a delicacy. It was a monstrosity.

Bray rolled with the nodding and pulled a pan out and set it on the stove to warm before making the offered sandwich, including all the meat options. Tevin, Jackson, and Finley shared a look. Except for Tevin, Bray made them all fend for themselves when they first arrived. And in Tevin's case, Bray expected Jackson to make sure Tevin ate, bathed, and didn't accidentally kill himself. AV (after Vixen) Bray was a lot nicer to be around than BV Bray.

"So, Foster?" Tevin plopped down in the chair across from the kid. "Why are you visiting Mac?"

Foster scrunched his nose and squinted his eyes at Tevin. Jackson didn't blame the kid.

"What the hell kind of question is that?" Finley appeared to be on Jackson and Foster's side of the debate on whether Tevin's question was stupid.

"What? We all wanna know. I mean, it's obvious, but short of convincing the kid to be quiet and evading Bray to listen in on Vixen's chat, Foster's the best source we have." Tevin explained his logic with the surety of someone confident that he made perfect sense.

Bray snorted as he stood in front of the stove, tending to the sandwich so the bread didn't burn. "Good luck with that."

"With what?" Tevin asked.

"All of that." Bray snorted again. Bray's frequent use of sarcasm was one of the less desirable side effects of Vixen's arrival.

Foster's head swiveled around the room, taking in all the sights and sounds. And smells too, if the crinkling of his nose gave any sign.

"How old are you, kid?" Jackson asked. The question was innocent, right? No one could accuse him of interrogating the kid.

Foster looked down at his hand. He straightened three fingers on one hand and bent a finger on his other hand before holding both up for Jackson to see. "This many."

"What is that? Four?"

Foster shook his head with such vigor his short blond hair did a half-assed impersonation of a shampoo ad. "Nooo. Thwee and this much" He held his hand out with the finger bent at the first knuckle.

Thwee? Jackson smiled at the way the kid worked his R's. It was hard not to think of Foster as cute. But then nature worked that way. Every pup, cub, kitten, or baby was cute. Bray said cuteness kept mothers and fathers from outright killing their offspring. There had to be some truth to Bray's theory. Tevin tried the patience of both Bray and Jackson yet lived.

"What? Is that like a half?" Jackson grinned down at Foster.

"Nooo. This much!" Foster shoved his nearly bent finger in Jackson's face, as if a closer view clarified things.

"Three quarters?" Bray got in on the guessing game as he placed a plate with a huge sandwich, big enough to feed any of the young men under his care, in front of Foster.

"Yeah. That many." Foster nodded, but he focused his attention on the sandwich in front of him. His little hands barely fit around the bread and there was no way his mouth was big enough to fit around the sandwich, but he looked determined to eat every bite.

Jackson counted back the years. Almost four years, plus another nine months. Or was it ten? Did it matter? Eleven years ago, when Jackson had just turned fifteen, by some bit of luck, Mac found Jackson and dropped him off at Bray's doorstep. And it was great living with Bray for a while. Until it wasn't.

Around five years ago, Jackson left Broken Peak and Bray's little pack. Jackson said it was permanent, but after a few months on his own, he came back. Bray's domineering ways were better than the world of humans. Apparently his brief vacation was long enough to become a dad.

But that still didn't explain not having any memory of the woman Foster called Mom. Yeah, Jackson had been drunk for a lot of those days during his break from Bray's domineering ways, but he hadn't been blackout drunk. He would have recognized her face. Or her scent. Especially her scent. Eleanor might not smell like fur, but she smelled like a heady mix of wild herbs and flowers that invaded the yard in the spring. Not that he paid attention to her scent, or the smell of the yard in spring, just that he'd remember it. Or that's what he told himself.

Jackson had been wandering some states west of the Mississippi right around the time Foster would have been conceived. But that still didn't explain Foster. Jackson was as certain he hadn't slept with Eleanor as he was the sun would rise in the morning.

He didn't doubt Foster was his, but Jackson didn't understand how Eleanor could be Foster's mom. She was a full-on human. Or at least she smelled human. Granted until Vixen came along, none of them bought into the latent myths that sprouted from shifters having kids with humans. Except, in all those stories, humans gave birth to latent offspring. Not shifters. But Foster, from his scent, was a wolf shifter.

"Where's your dad?" Finley asked

Foster lifted his head and stared across the table at Jackson. Saved by a mouthful of food, Foster didn't answer, but he didn't have to.

"Does your mom have a mate?" Jackson asked. He should have been focused on the kid, but at the moment he wanted to learn everything about Eleanor. Not that he understood the reasoning behind the urge to interrogate the almost four-year-old boy about his mother's relationships, just that his wolf encouraged him.

Foster shook his head, swallowed his food, and wiped the back of his hand across his mouth. "Nope. Just Mommy and me. Don't need anyone else." Foster narrowed his eyes at Jackson, daring the male to contradict him.

"You protect your mommy?" Bray asked. "Keep her safe?"

Foster bared his teeth and bobbed his head up and down.

A smiled cracked across Jackson's lips. Damn, his kid was cute with the way his wolf peeked out in response to Bray's question. As though the pup dared the bigger wolf to try anything.

Jackson glanced at the clock over the stove. Over twenty minutes had passed since the kid showed up in the kitchen claiming Vixen told him he could find food here and that Bray and the others should feed him. Did Jackson risk asking Foster about his wolf? With Jackson's luck, as soon as he opened his mouth, Vixen would come walking down the hallway and deliver a scathing lecture. And Eleanor would be there to witness it.

One thing he learned about Vixen, her lectures were worse than any training or stupid exercises she used for discipline when one of them disappointed her.

"So, did your mommy tell you why you came here?" If Foster shared he was a shifter, Jackson couldn't get in trouble for asking the kid about his wolf. No one had spoken the words aloud, but everyone knew Foster was a wolf.

"It's a secret. I'm not supposed to talk about it." Foster mumbled out through a full mouth.

Shiiiiit.

All the males shared a look. The first things a pup learned was to keep his mouth shut and his wolf hidden from humans. Foster uttered the same words they had all spoken when they met Mac or Bray for the first time.

"Hey Foster?" Bray sat down in a chair across from Jackson and Foster. "I have a secret too. And so does everyone here. How about I tell you my secret and if it's the same as yours, you'll know you can talk about it?"

Foster considered Bray's words and slowly nodded in agreement. There was no way the kid grasped the technicalities. Hell, Jackson had to go over the words several times before he figured out what Bray said. But if it got Foster to talk, Jackson didn't care.

"Something lives inside of me. And sometimes it comes out. Do you wanna know what it is?" Bray looked right at Foster and smiled as he let his eyes flash to a bright gold before returning to their natural brown.

Sandwich forgotten, Foster bobbed his head up and down so fast, Jackson worried the kid would snap his neck.

"I have a wolf inside of me."

"You do?" Foster whispered as his eyes grew to the size of his sandwich.

"I do. And do you know the best part about living here? My wolf can come out and run around as much as he wants. There's no one here we need to hide from."

Foster looked around the room then bent forward, leaning as close to Bray as the table allowed and whispered loudly, as only a little kid could, "I have a wolf too. But when he comes out, Mommy keeps him hidden."

Jackson swallowed back the lump in his throat. He had been so busy focusing on who Eleanor was and how Foster came to be that he didn't consider what it must have been like for a human to raise a wolf shifter. And if she had to keep him hidden, she didn't have any support. "Tell you what? Before you go to bed tonight, we'll have wolf time okay? Your wolf can run around with mine. No more hiding."

"You have a wolf too?" Foster hadn't put the pieces together yet and thought just Bray shared his secret.

"Yep. We all do. Everyone here in this room has a wolf. But we'll introduce you to them one at a time, okay? We don't want to frighten your wolf. So tonight it will just be me and Bray, okay?"

Again, Foster's head bobbed up and down. He picked his sandwich back up. Before taking a bite, he quietly repeated the word wolf time, and there was no mistaking the wonder in his voice.

CHAPTER NINE

ELEANOR and Vixen found Foster sitting at a table with five large men, including Jackson and Bray, all eating sandwiches the size of Foster's face.

Before Foster realized she was there, Vixen gently pulled Eleanor away and down a hallway that spurred off from the main passage. "See, he's fine."

"I know. I mean, I knew he would be, but I had to see it."

"Understandable. Now, we have enough room for both you and Foster to have your own rooms. But I think you'd prefer to be next to him?" Vixen asked and Eleanor nodded before Vixen continued on, "right, so, to make things easier, I'll move Tevin into another room and Foster can take his room."

"Oh. I don't want to be a problem."

"You aren't. But since Foster is young, I figured you'd want rooms closer to the common areas. Unless you don't?"

"No. But I'm not sure how long–"

"You're here as long as you want to be." Vixen stopped her quick pace, pivoted, and crossed her arms over her chest. Her steady gaze bore into Eleanor long enough to cause nervous fidgeting. "No one is going to make you leave. No one. Not for any reason."

Eleanor swallowed back the tears. She had been so alone for so long. Even before Foster and the shifting thing, Eleanor never had a real family.

Vixen gave Eleanor a nod, turned back around, and continued down the hall as though nothing had been said. Giving Eleanor the privacy she needed to gather her emotions and wrangle them back under control.

"Now, this is the room we use for guests since it has its own bathroom. But don't worry, we don't have guests." Vixen stood in front of an open door that led to a large bedroom decorated with rustic but functional furnishings. The only thing missing from the room was a window. "We're under the mountain. Bray's and my room is the only one with a window, but that's because it's the only bedroom not in the mountain. Your bags are here, but don't worry, we didn't unpack them. And if you need anything, be sure to tell me."

"I'm sure I won't need anything."

"From the size of your bags, you left more than you took." Vixen rested her hand against Eleanor's shoulder. "There's a shower and a bath. I had them add a decent bath after I moved in."

"Oh. Yes, thank you. I won't be long."

"Take your time. Foster is fine and from the size of that sandwich, it will take him a good fifteen minutes to finish. At which point, the boys will find something else for him to eat. Mac says he should hit his first growth spurt any day now and his stomach will become a bottomless pit."

"Vixen?" Eleanor pressed her hand against the doorjamb. "Thank you. For everything."

"It's what packs do." Vixen patted Eleanor's shoulder and gave her a gentle push into the bedroom before closing the door and leaving Eleanor alone.

The temptation of the hot shower was too great to resist and Eleanor stripped off her clothes on her way to the bathroom. She didn't even wait for the water to heat up before stepping into the shower. That's when the tears fell. The ugly cry she'd been holding back since Wayne pulled her away arrived with a vengeance. By the time she finished her crying jag, the water was cooling. She hurried through the motions of washing her hair and body before rinsing, turning off the water, and drying.

Eleanor pulled out some of her new clothes and wished she could wash them before wearing them. New clothes always had that chemical odor and the stiff fabric scratched her skin. She had left Foster alone for too long and didn't have time to fret about silly things like the comfort of jeans and a cheap long-sleeved shirt that wouldn't last three washes before falling apart.

With a deep breath she headed out of the room and turned toward the kitchen.

"Mommy!" Foster called from the table, waving at her with a chip-filled hand. "They have Cheetos!"

"And they're sharing them? Aren't you lucky?"

"Unca Bray gave me the entire bag!" Foster's eyes widened in pure glee.

Uncle? How long had she been in the shower? "Well, wasn't that nice of him? I hope you thanked him?"

Foster bobbed his head up and down. "And guess what, Mommy? I can talk about my wolf. And Vivi said I can see her special friend too someday, but not yet because it's not a wolf."

Eleanor fell back a step and Jackson, who'd been headed for the fridge, reached out to grab her before she fell over.

"Whoa, you okay?"

Eleanor looked up and Jackson grinned down at her. She closed her eyes to protect herself from the sight of the nearly perfect specimen of a man. Since Foster, there hadn't been anyone. No one. Not even a casual date despite the well-intentioned attempts of the department secretary. Eleanor made an excuse that she didn't have the time for a relationship, but the truth was she wasn't interested. Or at least she hadn't been interested. But that was before the image of the broad-shouldered and muscle bound gorgeous man imprinted on her retinas.

With a wink, as though he could tell where her thoughts had gone, Jackson settled Eleanor back on her feet and continued to the fridge. He pulled a gallon of milk from the fridge and poured a glass then set it down in front of Foster before sitting down next to him.

"You've already met Bray and Jackson. The others are Tevin, Finley, Allard, and Leighton. Don't worry, we don't expect you to figure out who is who yet." Vixen pushed away from the counter while pointing out the men as she said their names.

"And guess what Mommy?" Foster set the Cheetos down and picked up his glass of milk.

Eleanor stepped further into the kitchen while waving at unfamiliar faces. "What, baby?"

"We're going to have wolf time before bedtime!"

"You are?" She wasn't sure how she felt about Foster having wolf time, whatever wolf time meant. She wasn't even sure how she felt about everyone talking openly about wolves after spending four years of keeping it a secret.

Bray must have read the worry on her face. "He needs to learn how to control the shifts and the best way is to shift around those who can help him."

"I understand that," she lied, "it's just surprising is all."

Tevin, or maybe it was Finley, snorted and both Vixen and Bray reached out to smack whoever it was across the back of his head.

Jackson looked up and across the table at her with bright green eyes lighting up with amusement. "We're like Santa, we know when you're telling the truth."

"Oh..." Eleanor turned her head away and studied the kitchen appliances, doing her best to avoid the amused and knowing looks from the others in the room. Sitting in a room full of lie detectors wasn't on the top of Eleanor's list on how to spend an enjoyable evening. "Well, it is surprising."

"Bray has been making modified grilled cheeses where he stuffs whatever you want between the slices of bread. Would you like one?" Vixen asked.

"A grilled cheese sounds nice." Eleanor took another step into the kitchen.

"We have some soup heating too." Bray went to the stove and waited for Vixen to finish putting together the sandwich for him to grill.

Jackson stood halfway up and reached for Eleanor's wrist. He tugged her around the table and into the chair next to his. Her stomach shouldn't have done acrobatics and her heart shouldn't have sped up, but both happened. Jackson was a stranger. Her only tie to the man was an elephant in the room that no one acknowledged, but everyone assumed. Jackson was Foster's father, and she needed to do what was best for her son, which meant keeping things firmly in the friend area.

She could do this. For Foster's sake, she had to do this.

Vixen set a plate with a grilled cheese in front of Eleanor and Bray came from the other side with a bowl of soup.

"So when does this wolf time happen?" Eleanor asked as she tore a corner from her sandwich and chewed on it. "Should I race to finish eating, or can I take my time?"

Everyone in the room looked away from her except for Vixen. Apparently wolf shifters relied on similar avoidance tactics.

"You can take your time. Tonight it will be just the boys." Vixen sat down on Bray's knee and reached for a handful of potato chips.

"Oh." Eleanor stared down at her sandwich. The food that had tasted so good moments before, turned to cement in her mouth. She set the rest of the sandwich down on the plate and brushed the crumbs from her hands. No matter how kind or well-intentioned these people were, Eleanor was still Foster's mother. "It's been a long day for us. Maybe we should wait for wolf time."

"Mommmy." Foster dragged out the last syllable and extended the whine for several seconds longer. As though a longer whine could convince Eleanor to change her mind.

"Foster. I am not saying it won't happen. Just not tonight." Once Eleanor switched into mom gear, it was only a matter of seconds before she delivered her decision with a firm but reasonable mom voice. The one she began practicing when Foster learned the word no. "In the future, if you could please speak with me before making promises to my son."

When Eleanor looked around the room, she realized the lack of protests or excuses from the men had nothing to do with her and everything to do with the other woman in the room. Vixen's glare hit each and every man without her moving her head.

Eleanor needed to learn that trick.

CHAPTER TEN

A LOW growl rumbled from Jackson's chest. The news of not being able to meet with the pup upset his wolf. It was only the promise of being able to do it later that calmed the beast down enough so he'd stop pestering Jackson. To add to his wolf's frustration, Jackson understood Eleanor's reasoning. He didn't agree with it and planned to change her mind, but Eleanor wasn't being unreasonable. Which totally sucked.

"I just... It's just... If he's tired, Foster can get out of control sometimes. I think it's better for everyone if we wait for tomorrow." Eleanor dropped her hands to her lap and pulled the sleeves of her shirt down over her hands. "After a good night's sleep it's better."

Better. Not good. Better. What the hell were Foster's shifts like for Eleanor to use the word better? Without thinking, Jackson reached for her arm and pulled up her sleeve.

Shit.

Scars. Old scars, but still scars. There were even a few fresh scratches. "Eleanor..."

She was busy trying to pull her arm away and ignored the soft growl coming from Jackson. But Foster heard it.

Foster growled and snapped at Jackson.

Images of Tevin as an unruly pup flashed through Jackson's mind. "Eleanor, we'll talk about this later." He dropped her arm, stood, and picked Foster up by the back of his shirt and neck in a single motion.

Foster lifted his chin and glared at Jackson, but it was the wolf who glowered at Jackson, not the little boy.

Jackson gave the pup a shake and let his wolf push to the surface. It didn't matter if the kid stayed with the pack for a few hours, a few months, or a lifetime, Foster and his wolf had to learn about the ways of a pack and now was as good as any time to teach him.

"He's just scared." Eleanor was on her feet, pulling at Jackson's arm. "Please. Don't hurt him."

Foster bared his teeth and growled. It was a great growl too, full and rumbling, but cute as hell because it was still the growl of a pup. Foster's wolf didn't back down. Even if his arms and legs hung limply from the instinct of an adult holding a pup by the back of the neck, the pup hadn't accepted Jackson's dominance.

"I'm not going to hurt him, but he has to learn."

Jackson and Bray had done the same thing with Tevin, and Tevin weighed a lot more than the almost four-year-old. Jackson could stand in the kitchen holding Foster for hours if he needed to. And from the defiance in Foster's eyes, waiting hours was a strong possibility.

Vixen hurried around the table and wrapped an arm around Eleanor's shoulder, leading her away. "I promised you, no harm will come to you or Foster, Eleanor, but let's let the boys handle this for now."

Both Bray and Jackson recognized the frustrated anger of the pup and the fear of the boy. As much as Jackson wanted to tell Foster that all would be fine, he couldn't. An angry pup with fangs and claws would hurt someone if he felt threatened. The only reason for an uncontrolled shift, even if the one shifting was barely out of toddler-hood, was because the wolf felt it needed to protect Foster.

Bray tilted his head toward the hallway, "Finley."

"On it."

Finley and Tevin both jumped up from the table and raced through the house, closing doors as they went while Allard and Leighton made themselves scarce. The fewer wolves around, the better.

"I'll get the door, you get his shirt off." Bray didn't hesitate or stop to see if Jackson was behind Bray as he jumped from the table and raced down the hallway.

Jackson chased after Bray. He grabbed the bottom of Foster's shirt and yanked it off over the kid's head, while tucking Foster under his arm like a football. Wearing any clothes during a shift wasn't good for the animal, but wearing a shirt, especially a pup wearing a shirt, could end with the shirt choking the animal if he panicked. Pants, shoes, and socks tangled up legs and wounded pride, but weren't harmful.

Behind him, he heard Eleanor's pleas for Vixen to let her go. The sounds of concern coming from the human woman didn't make either his wolf or him happy, but for the moment Foster was his priority. He would deal with Eleanor later. After everyone calmed down.

Bray waited at the door, circling his arm as though that gesture would speed Jackson up. Both males raced against the clock. They didn't have much time to get out of the Lodge before Foster shifted. Fur tickled Jackson's palm, and he lengthened his stride. The second worst thing that could happen was for Foster to shift inside. A cornered pup in a strange place could hurt others and himself.

Jackson sped out the door and sent the fully shifted pup to the lawn with a gentle toss.

The pup rolled to his feet, growled, and then fell as Foster's jeans tangled around his back legs.

"One of us is gonna get nipped and puppy teeth are sharp as fuck. Roshambo you to see who has to wade in and get his pants off?" Bray stared down at the snarling pup.

Yep. Foster's wolf was a pissant.

Jackson lifted his fist. "Two out of three?"

Jackson lost. The pants ended up not being the problem. The removal of the Spiderman underwear, however, required both Bray and Jackson.

Once free, Foster raced around the yard in tight circles. With his bottom tucked underneath him, he sped between Bray and Jackson, who blocked the pup from getting back into the house. Both Foster and the pup wanted Eleanor. Jackson didn't have to look too closely at the situation to read into the reason for the pup's attempts to break back into the Lodge. But Bray and Jackson wouldn't leave the other alone to handle the frightened pup while they returned to Vixen attempting to calm Eleanor, who was as panicked as Foster.

Shifting wasn't an option either. A large dominant male might spook the pup. If that happened, it wouldn't be a snarling pup with sharp teeth nipping at their ankles, it would be a frightened pup racing through the forest in the dark and definitely getting hurt. Jackson imagined the pain and hurt in Eleanor's eyes as he explained why they had to get a search party together when it was dark outside to locate a missing pup and decided he would do everything in his power to prevent that from happening.

Foster tired of charging at Jackson and Bray's ankles to break through the barrier their legs made after more attempts than Jackson wanted to count. The pup wasn't willing to cede the body to the boy though and was currently exploring the yard. Each blade of grass needed sniffing and every leaf, bush, and tree needed peeing on.

Jackson watched the explorations and wondered how he spent four years as a dad and didn't know. He wondered if it would have made a difference. Would he have stayed in Missouri, Arkansas, or Oklahoma or wherever the hell he had been when he knocked up Foster's mom or would he have run back to Bray sooner?

And how the hell had Eleanor kept anyone from learning Foster was a shifter? How had it not hit the news? From the scratches and scars on her arms, the shifts weren't easy for either of them. Regardless, if Eleanor planned on staying or not, Foster had to stay. If they let Foster leave, he'd either hit the evening news because of an uncontrolled shift or hurt someone.

Anxiety invaded. No other way to explain the sweaty palms and racing heart that arrived as soon as he thought about Eleanor.

"If we had any doubts, from the amount of scratches and bites on our hands, he's yours." Bray broke their silence as he watched the pup hopping after a toad.

The pup looked back over his shoulder at both Bray and Jackson. From the flailing legs hanging from the pup's mouth, he caught the toad. Before either of them could stop Foster, the wolf pup tilted his head back and chomped down three times before the toad slid down his gullet.

"That is not going to be pretty coming back up." Bray observed.

Jackson rubbed the outside corners of his eyes with his thumb and middle finger of his right hand. The kid was going to be ten times more trouble than Tevin ever was.

"Maybe it won't come back up?" Jackson added with a tinge of wishful thinking.

Bray snorted. "Yeah, when has anything like that ever stayed down?"

He had a point. While adult wolves hunted and enjoyed fresh game without any discomfort to their human counterparts, pups didn't seem to enjoy that same luxury. With the toad consumed, the pup looked around for something else to stalk and practice pouncing on.

Foster's wolf mauled the fallen leaves in the yard, only moving on after he shredded the leaf into tiny pieces. With Foster's wolf cleaning up the yard for them, they wouldn't have to worry about Vixen making them get a rake out. Jackson tilted his head to the side and watched the playing pup. "He's definitely mine. I counted back the days, and it makes sense, but I still don't remember the woman."

"Vixen's got her story and will fill us in when she thinks we need to know."

Bray was certain of his mate and it was a nice side to see in the Alpha. But it did nothing to ease the growing ache in Jackson's chest. He rubbed his fist up and down his sternum. The rubbing didn't ease the ache either. "Not that I don't trust your mate, Bray. I just don't like her timetable."

"Yeah, she's annoying like that." Bray leaned forward on the porch railing. "He's calmer now. I'll stand guard of the door while you shift then I'll head back inside and help keep Eleanor busy before she bursts out here."

"You don't think it's too soon?"

"Nope. Like Mac and Vixen say, rip it off like a band-aid."

Jackson's wolf perked up. He'd been wanting to come out since they saw Foster for the first time at Mac's cottage. Jackson stripped off his clothes and surrendered his body to the wolf. The change happened in an instant. One moment Jackson the man was standing on the front porch and the next, a light colored wolf stood over the pile of clothes. No pain. No sparkling lights. No loud pop.

It happened so fast, the pup hadn't even noticed the change. He did, however, notice the new scent. Well not new exactly, Jackson, Foster, Bray, and every other shifter had the same scent whether they were walking on two legs or four, but the scent grew stronger when shifted. The pup noticed it and decided he wanted nothing to do with the bigger wolf.

Bray laughed as Foster ran toward the woods. "He is definitely yours and from all the shit you gave me, you deserve everything he's going to give you."

Jackson gave Bray a friendly, if slightly annoyed, growl before trotting after the fleeing puppy.

Foster was fast. Much faster than a pup with short legs should be. But this was Foster's first experience with an adult and instinct told him he needed to stay clear of a dominant male. Jackson lost sight of the pup several times, but never lost the pup's scent.

The pup headed to the river. Jackson leapt over fallen logs and tore through the bushes, speeding after Foster before he got close to the shore. It wouldn't matter whether Foster managed an approximation of a dog paddle, the current was strong enough to pull the pup under. With Foster already fleeing because of discovering an adult wolf close by, the fast water of the river would send him into a full-blown panic.

Despite all of Jackson's efforts, he was too late. He found the pup yelping and whining in the middle of the river, the current spinning him in circles while he did his best to keep his head above water.

Shit.

Jackson waded into the river. The water was deep enough to lap against his chest and stomach, but he didn't lose his footing. A small blessing. If he had to swim and drag Foster from the river, he'd be having a much different conversation with Eleanor when they returned to the Lodge.

The wolf took over, ignoring Jackson's instinct to immediately go after the pup. Instead, he headed further down river, waded out as far as he could go without losing his footing, and waited. Jackson pushed against his wolf's control, the need to splash against the current and get to the struggling pup overwhelming the man. The wolf rarely pushed against Jackson's control, but this time the beast stood firm and refused to relinquish his body.

Foster floated down the river, spinning slowly, his howls growing louder, although Jackson couldn't tell if the louder volume was from the ever increasing panic or because the pup was drawing closer. Right before Jackson yanked his wolf back inside, Foster came bobbing along the river. The wolf clamped down on the nape of the pup's neck and pulled him out of the water while backing up to the shoreline. As nature designed it, Foster went limp but continued to whimper.

Trotting away from the river, Jackson knew he couldn't get back to the Lodge before Foster went into shock. Both he and his wolf had explored the woods and knew of the perfect spot. A shallow den under a dead tree that had fallen over and uprooted itself. It wasn't too far away and the perfect place to calm the pup down before heading back to the Lodge.

Jackson dropped Foster to the ground, made soft with dried pine needles, and placed a paw across the puppy's back to hold him in place. Jackson began bathing Foster with long slow licks. Foster shivered, but at least he didn't pull away. Jackson sat down, blocking the entry to the den with his body and continued washing Foster.

The whimpering stopped and Foster rolled over on his back, baring his belly in submission to Jackson. The wolf stopped his ministrations and looked up at the moon. They'd been gone longer than Jackson thought, and Bray could only keep Eleanor occupied for so long before she insisted they put together a search party to find her runaway son.

If Foster had been raised in a pack and experienced shifting with other wolves, Jackson would have comforted him enough to calm him down before heading back to the Lodge with the expectation that Foster would follow.

Foster turned his head toward Jackson's foreleg and mouthed at the leg. Jackson the man, who watched from behind the wolf's eyes, laughed. The wolf even chuffed out a low growl. The pup wanted to play. Perhaps tomorrow, when they had the entire day to explore the world as wolves, but right now, Jackson needed to get Foster home to keep Eleanor from losing her mind.

Jackson gave Foster a nudge with his nose then turned and walked down the path. He hoped the pup would follow, or he'd have to carry Foster back home and neither adult wolf nor pup would enjoy that. Jackson didn't need to worry. Foster ran after him. And promptly rolled into Jackson's back legs as he lost control of his own little legs. Jackson laughed again as his wolf stopped, lowered his head and looked down between his legs at the puppy twisting about to regain his footing. Jackson barked low, and the pup sat back on his haunches with his back legs splayed out to the side.

Another bark and Foster stood up with his tail wagging. Together they walked through the woods back to the Lodge with Jackson nudging Foster along when something new and exciting distracted the pup. As they came out of the woods, Bray, Vixen, and Eleanor waited for them.

Foster spotted Eleanor first and took off as fast as his little legs could carry him. Jackson continued behind at a more leisurely pace. He didn't want to frighten Eleanor. In fact, Jackson wanted the exact opposite. Both man and wolf wanted to impress the woman.

As Foster neared Eleanor, the pup's hackles raised and his tail ceased its side-to-side motion. Gone was the carefree pup who after a bit of a scare settled into the world newly open to him. Jackson couldn't get to the Lodge in time, but Bray was already stepping in front of Eleanor while Vixen pulled her back closer to the front door.

Bray had access to his Alpha strength as both man and wolf. Instead of shifting and sending the pup away in a panic, he stood at the bottom of the steps and glared down at Foster. The little pup ignored the weight that even Jackson felt from several yards away and continued to growl and snarl in his puppy way. Cute as hell because it was a pup, but Foster had a pile of bad manners that needed correcting and Jackson needed to do the correcting, not Bray.

Jackson picked up his pace and trotted the rest of the distance to Foster. As soon as he reached the pup, he planted a paw down on the pup's back, lowered his head, and growled low into Foster's ear.

The pup got the message in a matter of seconds and rolled to his back to give Jackson his belly. Jackson kept his muzzle close to the pup's, daring Foster to try to be cute and chew on his leg like he did earlier. Jackson was disciplining the pup, not comforting him. There would be time enough later for comforting.

"Go on. You should greet Foster's wolf. Get to know each other all over again." Vixen pushed Eleanor down the steps with a gentle shove, before grabbing Bray's hand and pulling him inside with her. "They don't need us here."

Jackson lifted his head and huffed out a low bark in thanks. Vixen looked over her shoulder and winked while giving Jackson a thumbs up. The woman might have been a cold-blooded assassin with a monster of an animal living inside her, but she could also be a goof when the situation warranted it. He needed to thank Vixen later. Even if Jackson had all his talks with Bray, Jackson knew Vixen was the reason Bray could have those talks.

Jackson swiveled his head and studied Eleanor, who stood at the base of the steps and from the size of her eyes and her open mouth, looked as though she was about to run in the opposite direction as fast as her legs could carry her. Huffing out a loud breath that might have been a sigh, he lifted his nose toward her without lifting his paw from Foster. The pup wasn't happy, but oh well. He needed to learn and now was as good of time as any.

"Um, hello?" She did a good job of hiding the tremble in her voice, but she couldn't keep her nerves hidden.

Jackson smelled her anxiety. It wasn't fear, but it was close to it. If this was what she was like when Foster shifted, no wonder his wolf was such a pissant. He lifted his paw, but snapped at the pup when Foster darted for Eleanor. Jackson wouldn't have blamed her if she stepped away, but she held her ground.

Brave mate.

What?

No.

Brave woman, Jackson corrected his wolf.

Another step closer to Eleanor and another sharp snap and firm growl for Foster. It took longer than Jackson would have liked, but eventually Foster stopped nipping at everyone. Jackson sat down in front of her.

The next move was in Eleanor's hands. Jackson couldn't force her to touch or pet him, but he did his best to appear less wolf like and more dog-like. He tilted his head to the side and let his tongue loll out of his mouth. Sure, his wolf might stand at the same height as Eleanor and when sitting down, he didn't need to tilt his head back to look at her, but he could do unassuming and cute.

Eleanor reached out and pressed her hand against Jackson's chest. "Jackson?"

Jackson let out another huff, but it was closer to a chuff this time.

She looked down at the pup who was belly-crawling his way closer to Jackson. "He looks just like you. As a wolf and a boy."

Jackson looked down at Foster, who crept his way in between Jackson's front legs and now sat underneath the adult wolf. What do you know? Foster did look like him. Jackson lifted his head and leaned forward. Before Eleanor freaked out and ran, Jackson ran his tongue along her cheek.

Salt. Eleanor had been crying. Before Vixen, Jackson had thought all tears were bad, but Vixen taught him sometimes they could be good. Jackson hoped this was one of those times when tears were good.

Foster whined, Eleanor gave a soft laugh and a sniff, and Jackson bent his head down, pushing the pup forward with his muzzle.

Eleanor crouched down and Foster belly crawled the short distance to her feet. Before Jackson had to remind the pup about his manners, Foster rolled over on his back and wriggled in the grass. Eleanor's laughter grew from a soft hesitant noise to a full-blown laugh that echoed throughout the yard. She reached down and dug her fingers into Foster's belly.

Satisfied, Jackson lay down and stretched his large body out while keeping an eye open to watch Foster. Mom and pup needed some alone time, but until Jackson trusted that Foster's wolf understood Eleanor's role, Jackson would keep a watchful eye on the pup.

CHAPTER ELEVEN

ELEANOR sat in the middle of the bed with her legs crossed and Foster still in wolf form curled up in her lap. Jackson was in the room too, also in wolf form, sprawled out on the floor. Jackson was a large man and his wolf was also large. He took up most of the floor and the room wasn't small by anyone's standards.

She stroked her fingers through Foster's fur, something she hadn't been able to do without coming away with scratches and bite marks since Foster was a baby.

"When the hospital called and told me about my sister, I almost hung up on them."

The enormous wolf rolled his body, so he lay on his stomach and lifted his head with his ears perked forward.

"The last thing I wanted or needed was to clean up another one of my sister's messes. When I arrived at the hospital, I planned on telling her she was on her own. That I didn't care what she did, and to remove me as her emergency contact."

Jackson slid across the floor, his claws scratching against the hardwood as he moved closer to her.

"And then I saw him." Eleanor looked down at the sleeping pup and smiled. "Wrapped up like a burrito with his scrunched-up face. Even then, he looked nothing like our side of the family. But he opened his eyes and looked at me. I know he wasn't looking at me, that all he saw was a blob, but at that moment, I like to think he saw me. And I *knew*. I knew he had to go home with me. I didn't care what my sister did, but that little boy was mine."

Jackson inched closer until he was next to her. He sat up and rested his head on top of the bed, next to her knee. Eleanor reached over and scratched between his ears.

"I was so scared. My mom isn't a great example of a mother, and I didn't get to experience any of the good things about pregnancy like the glowing skin," Eleanor looked down at her chest, "or a visit from the boob fairy. I also didn't get to experience any of the bad things either though. No constant peeing, no gas, no odd memory loss.

"I had just graduated from college. Planned to go to graduate school. I still went, but took longer than my peers. Foster changed my entire life." Eleanor looked down at Foster in her lap, one hand still on Jackson's head and the other pressed against Foster's chest, feeling his heart beat against her palm. "If I had the opportunity to go back, I wouldn't change a thing." Eleanor scratched at Jackson's head and the wolf's eyelids dropped until his eyes were almost closed. "Even the reason for coming here. Because without it, I wouldn't have this. I wouldn't get the chance for Foster's wolf to sleep on my lap. He was frightened and hurting me too, but I didn't know how to fix it. You fixed it for me. So thank you."

The wolf placed one paw on the bed. Then another. And another and another until all four legs were on the bed. He didn't give Eleanor a choice before he circled around and lay down behind her, curling his body around both woman and pup.

"Oh. Well." Eleanor giggled. Actually giggled. She hadn't giggled in years. Not even when she was a girl in high school when all girls giggled. "I hope the bed is reinforced. You're a large man, but you're an even bigger wolf. Is that why Jackson is so big? To have enough room for your wolf?"

With the warmth from the wolf at her back and the puppy in her lap, Eleanor closed her eyes and leaned back against the wolf. He snuffed at her ear and neck until she curled up on her side, tucking Foster against her stomach.

The day had been long for Eleanor. It seemed as though it was years ago that she woke up in the morning and drove the final leg of the journey to the Appalachians. It wasn't even tomorrow and Foster had a dad. Even if no one outright said as much, Eleanor and Foster had a safe place to stay, and Eleanor didn't need to worry when Foster's wolf made a surprise appearance.

Eleanor's eyes grew heavy and soon her breathing matched the pup's as sleep caught up with her.

WITHOUT THE CLOCK ON THE NIGHTSTAND, ELEANOR WOULDN'T HAVE known it was well past nine o'clock in the morning when she woke up. She never slept in. Foster was always up at the crack of dawn and if she didn't get up with him, he'd make a mess of the kitchen preparing breakfast and destroy the bathroom getting ready for the day. She never had the heart to get upset with him, since he didn't mean to cause trouble, so instead Eleanor woke up with him.

Foster must have been more worn out than she thought for him to still be asleep. Eleanor reached her arms over her head and pointed her toes in a morning stretch, then rolled over expecting to find Foster still asleep. Instead, her face ran into the bare chest of a man.

"Mmmph." Planting her hands against his very firm abdomen, she pushed herself back and sat up.

Jackson, head perched on his hand with his elbow bent and resting on the bed looked up at her with a grin. "Vixen said to let you sleep. She came and got Foster, said something about having a task for him. If he's lucky, it will be an obstacle course, if he's unlucky, he'll be running laps through the forest."

"Oh. I should get up and check on him. He's..."

"He shifted back in the middle of the night. I'm guessing his wolf was too excited to give up control. Bray or I can force changes, but his wolf needed the time with you."

Eleanor rolled away from Jackson and out of bed. Everyone else might be okay with taking her son off for fun romps, but she definitely wasn't. Not yet at least.

As soon as her feet hit the floor, and she stood up, she realized she wasn't wearing pants. She might have been tired the night before, but she would have remembered taking them off. She spun around the room, but couldn't find them anywhere.

"Vixen also took your jeans. I took them off last night. After you fell asleep because sleeping in jeans is uncomfortable as fuck, but Vixen said she needed them for your size."

"Oh." Eleanor needed to find a dictionary and expand her vocabulary. She also needed to find a pair of pants. Pulling her shirt down until it covered all of her bits, she crouched down and pulled out a pair of pants from her bag.

She reached in and grabbed whatever her hand found that was pant like. If she had paid any attention, she would have discovered the pants she grabbed had a word written across the butt. Seeing as they were from a discount store, the name attempted to mimic a popular brand, but failed on all counts. Jelly. Her ass was jelly according to her pants.

She pulled up the pants and turned to face a grinning Jackson.

"They were in the bargain bin."

"I didn't say anything."

"You didn't need to. I would have returned them if I had realized." Eleanor planted her hands on her hips and surveyed the room. Even if she was only staying for a few days, she should unpack and use the space to hold her limited selection of clothing. And if Foster had his own room, she'd need to put his things there. Foster was particular about keeping his things in his room. She had never been sure if it was a little boy thing, a wolf thing, or both.

"Well, you want to talk about it now, or pretend we talked about it so Vixen stops bothering us. She hasn't told me anything, just that we need to talk. Which is why I think she took Foster, to give us time alone." Jackson rolled onto his back and folded his arms behind his neck, making his chest even broader than it was as his muscles flexed.

"There's a lot to talk about."

"Well, Vixen would call it the 600 pound gorilla that's leering at us from the corner and not going to go away just because we ignore it."

"In all fairness, there's a bunch of 600 pound gorillas in the room right now."

"A whoop?"

"A what?"

"It's what we call a group of gorillas."

Eleanor fell down on the bed, needing something to support her legs. "There are weregorillas?"

"Shifters. And, yeah. There are all kinds of shifters, some don't even exist in the wild. In the wild gorillas are usually called troops, but gorilla shifters are the most peaceful shifters and call themselves whoops."

"Okay, first, that's really cool, and I'm going to have a lot of questions about that later. But let's go back to the 600 pound gorilla you mentioned."

"Woman, are you going to make me say it?"

Eleanor nodded. She had an inkling what it would be about, but wanted confirmation before she opened her mouth.

"Well, I think we both know Foster is my kid. And I'm over the whole you not telling me I was a father when I became one."

Eleanor raised her hand, stopping Jackson from continuing. "Until a few days ago, I didn't even know your name. And Foster is my son, but I adopted him. From my sister."

Jackson closed his eyes and released a loud breath. "Thank God, cause, El, I gotta tell you, I didn't remember you and I'd like to think I wouldn't have forgotten you. There's still a bit of a sticky wicket though."

"Sticky wicket?" Those two words sounded odd coming from Jackson's mouth.

Jackson shrugged. "Vixen uses it a lot. Guess I picked it up from her. But we have a sticky wicket, because shifters and humans have latents, and Foster isn't a latent. That kid has a full-on little shit of a wolf inside of him. But you aren't a latent."

"Wait, how can you tell?"

"Cause we can. Well, it's more Bray, Vixen, Mac, and I are convinced you aren't."

"Why are you so sure I don't have a wolf inside me too? There has to be something more than a feeling or gut instinct." Eleanor's researcher side came to the forefront and demanded quantifiable answers.

"It's a mix of things. A scent. Like calling to like. Our animals would recognize an animal inside you, even if she's latent. Like we didn't know what Vixen was, we couldn't recognize her animal until Bray freed it, but we knew she wasn't human."

Eleanor's eyes widened. There was a mystery at Broken Peak, one that looked to be right up Eleanor's alley. If she couldn't convince them to keep her and Foster for Foster's sake, maybe Eleanor could convince them she could help.

"Long story and one you'll hear about when you meet Vixen's animal. And now that we know Foster isn't yours—"

"Whoa. Foster is one hundred percent mine. In the eyes of the law, he is mine. A judge even signed a decree, a legal document, that created a parent child relationship between Foster and me, as though he was my biological child. He. Is. Mine."

Jackson's forehead crinkled as he considered Eleanor's words. Foster made the same expression when she introduced a new concept to him.

"Okay. Not gonna argue with that, but I don't think the decree, or whatever it is, took his wolf into consideration. If you were a latent, you'd have better control over his pup, even if your wolf was asleep, Foster's pup would still respond to her. So, you're a full-on human."

"And that makes me a terrible mom?"

"Woman, did I say that? No. Just that, well, Foster's mine and I don't think we need one of those paternity tests to verify that he is. Like it or not, his wolf needs to learn manners from a pack."

"I'm not giving Foster up. You can't take him away from me." Eleanor jumped to her feet, but Jackson grabbed her wrist and pulled her back to the bed before she walked away from him in a huff.

"No one is saying that, woman. El, you have got to stop jumping to all these confounded conclusions, it's making this all more complicated than it has to be."

She shouldn't have liked the way he shortened her name or the way he kept his hand on her, drawing small circles on the inside of her wrist. The familiarity distracted her from what they should be focused on. Foster. Her son was her priority. Not the way Jackson made her stomach flutter or her heart race.

"El, are you sure your sister and you have the same dad?" Jackson rolled over and moved her around so he held her hand between both of his.

"Well, no. It's possible. Even likely that we had different fathers. Our mother wasn't very selective when it came to allowing men access to her vagina. I guess we just assumed we had the same dad since our mother never mentioned two different dads. Why?"

"If your sister's father was a shifter, then your sister's a latent, then Foster being a wolf makes a lot more sense. Though, I still don't remember her."

"What do you mean?"

"Doesn't she look like you? Cause darlin', there's no way I'd forget your sister if she looked even a little like you."

Jackson's words sounded like a compliment. Sort of. If she looked at it upside down with both eyes closed. "I guess, if we're standing next to each other, we're similar enough to be sisters, but no one ever came up and told me I reminded them of someone and it turned out it was my sister."

Jackson rolled to his back and brought Eleanor with him, pressing her against his body. Normally, Eleanor would think he was being too forward, but after his wolf cuddled against her the night before, she figured this was just a wolf thing. When his fingers combed through her hair and a low hum came from him, she was *convinced* it was a wolf thing.

"So. I'm a dad."

"And I'm his mom."

"I know. Just let me have the dad thing for a few minutes, okay? Then I promise to give back the mom thing."

"Jackson, that's not what—"

"I know. Look, I don't know what Vixen said to you, but I talked with Bray. You and Foster, you both can stay as long as you want. And I want you to. Both my wolf and I want you to stay."

THE NEXT FEW DAYS PASSED EVEN FASTER THAN THE DAY ELEANOR AND Foster arrived at Broken Peak. Eleanor spent her mornings making Foster breakfast. She also learned to make ten times as much food because everyone else wandered into the kitchen, following the scent of food, and she'd feed them as well.

Inevitably Foster and Jackson headed off to do wolf things, Bray and the others did whatever they did, and Vixen gave Eleanor the space she needed to get more comfortable. At first, Eleanor explored the lodge. Once she learned the layout, she spent her time in the kitchen cooking, in the main room, reading, or outside on the porch swing. She'd never had as much freedom before, but all the men in the pack found reasons to spend time with Foster. The little boy was getting a crash course on having a wolf and Eleanor had never seen him happier.

On the third day, Mac found Eleanor swinging on the front porch with a blanket wrapped around her legs and the old journal Wayne had shoved in her bag when he pulled her from the study room.

"What have you got there?" The older man shuffled across the porch and sat down next to Eleanor on the swing.

"A journal." She didn't look up from the page she was studying. A small mark next to a name confused her. She couldn't tell if it was a deliberate shape or a blob of ink. Once she identified the special marks, she found several more ink blobs, enough for Eleanor to think they were deliberate and intended to confuse anyone reading the journal pages.

Mac pulled the brim of his hat down over his eyes and stretched his legs out in front of him, crossing them at the ankles. "You don't say."

"How come I get the feeling that you know exactly what I have." Eleanor lifted her head and looked at Mac with a slight grin. He was a cagey old codger who liked to play up the frail old man image, but Eleanor wasn't buying any of it.

He reached into his coat and pulled out a twin to the journal, setting it down on her lap. "Wayne said you were studying folklore." His gnarled finger tapped at the cover of the journal. "That's not folklore."

"I'm studying magic as it pertains to remedies and treatments in American Folklore." She didn't dare ask why Mac had a journal that matched the one she stole from the University.

"It's not magic. Not in the way you're studying. It's magic in the way shifters are magic."

"How d'you know?

"Wayne told me he was sending it with you and you didn't know what you found, but once you told him about it, he began planning how to steal it." Mack pushed the book further into her lap. "No idea how it went missing, or even that it was missing. We're usually better about keeping our secrets secret."

"Mac..." How had she not put it together when she met Mac for the first time?

"Short for MacAllister. Yeah. Edna was a great-great grandmother of mine. She was also a crazy coot. Lived on her own after her husband died and didn't turn anyone away who showed up at her door. Shifter or human." Mac tucked his chin against his chest. "She would have opened her house to you and yours."

"Is that why you do what you do? Because of Edna?"

Mac chuffed out a loud laugh. "Nah, I help when I can because I'm a last resort. This pack right here? All needed a last resort."

"Even Vixen?"

"Vixen more than anyone else. By the way, you made an impression on her."

"On who? Vixen?"

"She might not have told you as much, but you are hers and that means she'll protect you. No matter what happens."

"Mac, why are you telling me this?"

"Well, just in case you get any strange ideas about leaving, I want you to know what you'll be leaving behind."

"Why do you think I'll leave?"

"Lass, I've seen that look before. You're feeling safe. No stories in the news about a little boy who's a werewolf. No emergency calls from Wayne or Victor. You think it's safe to go back. And it might be, but that don't mean it's good for you or your boy." Mac pushed the brim of his hat up and winked at Eleanor. "It's almost the end of October. I don't imagine there's a good neighborhood for tricking-or-treating around here, but I bet Roose and me could load up on enough candy that Foster can go back and forth for a while before he gets bored."

Halloween. How could she have forgotten? Eleanor's mind ran away with ideas. Maybe she could even convince the others to dress up and make a thing of it. "I'll need to get him a costume..."

Mac patted his hand on top of her legs in that grandfatherly way of his. "Vixen has a direct line with Amazon. I'm sure she can find something for Foster and the other boys. Now, lass, if you'll excuse me, I need to find Vixen."

"You didn't come just to talk with me."

"Nope. I came because Vixen found me a whiskey column for my still, and I wanted to check if it arrived." Mac pushed off the swing and shuffled into the house as though he belonged there.

Once he disappeared inside the house, Eleanor couldn't resist diving into the new journal. Edna's remedies included an interesting mix of common sense still in practice today and off-the-wall treatments. Her patient notes were an interesting blend of symptoms and commentary, and worth the read.

CHAPTER TWELVE

THE days slipped into a week, and the week approached two weeks. Both Eleanor and Foster fell into the ways of the pack. Foster and Jackson had their wolf time. When the days got away from them and the wolf time was after dinner, but before bed, Jackson and Foster's wolves would creep into her room and fall asleep as wolves but wake up as a man and a boy. Eleanor figured Vixen must have some kind of super sense because on those mornings, Foster spent time with either Vixen or Bray and Eleanor woke up with Jackson in her bed. Not that anything happened, although, if she thought about it, she wouldn't turn Jackson away.

Jackson with the shaggy blond hair he was always brushing out of his eyes and the broad shoulders and arm muscles that threatened the integrity of his shirts. Jackson with the cheekbones and jawline that belonged on a man who graced the covers of a magazine instead of a man far removed from civilization. Jackson with the easy smiles when he thought no one was looking and the bright green eyes that followed Foster's every move.

Eleanor often caught him watching Foster, letting the boy learn and explore on his own, but ready to run in and prevent a tragedy. Like the time Foster decided he wanted to climb a tree. The others encouraged the boy and Foster made it halfway up a lodgepole pine before Eleanor found him and Foster realized he had to climb back down. While the others came up with Rube Goldberg contraptions to get the boy down, Jackson climbed up to Foster then helped him reach the ground with no broken bones.

Jackson was a wonderful dad. They still hadn't said anything explicit to Foster, but Jackson was the first one Foster looked for when he had something to share or wanted an audience while he read a book.

"Okay, I found the perfect costumes, but need confirmation." Vixen plopped down on the porch swing next to Eleanor and shoved a laptop into Eleanor's face.

"Um, I'm not sure Foster is the right age for a biker."

"That's not a biker. Think less outlaw and more late 70s early 80s disco scene. And that's not for Foster."

"Oh... Oh!" Eleanor squinted her eyes at the screen. "Well, I guess if we're throwing political correctness out the window."

"Yeah, but imagine all six of them in tight fitting, chest baring, wholly inappropriate costumes that we can convince them to wear because the costumes are the epitome of masculinity."

"You can get them to agree to wear them?"

"Easy peasy."

"We'll need speakers."

"Why?" Vixen scrolled through the screen, ogling the male models in their costumes.

"Because I will want *YMCA* and *Macho Man* playing in the background and it's not going to be enough to sing it to myself."

"Fair enough. And I found the perfect costume for you too."

"Me? Why do I need a costume?"

"Because it will be easier to convince the boys to dress up if we're dressed up too."

"Oh? You're dressing up too?"

"Of course."

"What did you find for Foster?"

"Is a wolf costume too on the nose?"

"Oh my God, is that Pete the Cat?" Eleanor pointed at the blue costume with a yellow jacket.

"Who?"

"Haven't you heard Foster singing about different colored shoes? Pete's his favorite book and song."

"Well then, he needs to be Pete the Cat." Vixen added the costume to her shopping cart.

"You aren't going to tell me what costume you got for me?" Eleanor asked.

"Nope. You aren't getting a chance to say no."

"Were the costumes your only reason for talking with me?"

"What? Like I need a reason to corner you and offer you unsolicited advice?" Vixen took the laptop back and completed her purchases. "You and Jackson need a date night."

"Why do we need a date night?"

"Are you blind? Have you not noticed the way he stares at you when he thinks you aren't looking, and with that goofy grin of his too."

"He's not staring at me. He's looking at Foster."

"Keep telling yourself that, sweetheart, and you might just believe it someday." Vixen hugged the closed laptop to her chest and stretched her legs out in front of her. "Your sister has no interest in Foster?"

"Wouldn't matter if she did, but no."

"She doesn't know what she's missing out on. He's a great kid. And I don't even like kids all that much, so that's saying something."

Eleanor snorted and covered her mouth to hide the noise.

"When I first came here, one of them, I can't remember who, wanted my opinion on motherhood. I think they liked the concept of having something little to distract Bray. At the time they hadn't put two and two together to realize I could distract Bray just fine without a pup running around."

"I'd like to think she gave up Foster because it was best for him. But that wasn't why. She gave him up because it was best for her."

"She sounds like a real peach." Vixen wrapped her arm around Eleanor's shoulder and gave her a side hug. "Even though I never met her, I don't like her. Inevitably, Foster would have found his way here because Mac has some secret super power that pulls shifters here, but there's no way she would have fit in as well as you have."

"Mac has a secret super power?"

Vixen threw her head back and laughed. It wasn't a polite laugh, but one of those infectious loud sounds that invited anyone within hearing distance to join. "No. But wouldn't it be cool if he did? On our way here from Mac's, on your first day, Bray told Jackson both you and Foster were welcome to stay. From what you've told me about her, he wouldn't make that same offer to your sister.

"Yeah. I wouldn't make the same offer either."

CHAPTER THIRTEEN

JACKSON leaned back in his chair and surveyed the rest of the pack sitting around the dinner table chatting away about nothing and everything. Foster and Eleanor had slipped into the patterns of day-to-day life as though they'd always been there. His wolf didn't frighten Eleanor, and Jackson had long given up on convincing his wolf to shift back after Foster and Jackson did their wolf things at night before bedtime. His wolf looked as forward to Eleanor's talks as Eleanor seemed to.

Foster reached across his plate for the large glass of milk and his elbow hit the cutlery. Before it fell to the ground, Jackson caught the knife and fork and set them back on Foster's plate. The kid didn't need silverware to eat the mammoth brownie Vixen served him, but Vixen was using a knife and fork so Foster insisted he needed them too.

"Foster? Do you have a tummy ache? You ate a lot today." Eleanor licked her napkin before wiping it across Foster's face, cleaning off most the brownie crumbs clinging around his mouth, cheeks, and chin. Foster even had crumbs in his eyebrows.

"Nope," Foster took another long drink before carefully setting the glass down.

"He's probably about to hit a growth spurt soon. Since it's his first, it will happen in short bursts over months." Jackson slid the knife away from the edge of the plate it had crept up on with the help of Foster's elbow. "Vixen, we should add clothes to your shopping list. I don't think even Tevin's smallest stuff will fit him yet."

"Oh, he doesn't need new clothes. When we left Missouri, I bought clothes a few sizes too big."

Jackson grinned. "It's cute you think he'll only go up a few sizes with his first growth. Woman, he's going to be the size of a kid twice his age when his first spurt finishes. Then he'll have little spurts until puberty. When he hits twelve or thirteen, we're going to have to double our normal Costco order."

"Thirteen? That's like ten years from now."

"Nine," Vixen corrected Eleanor with a sly grin.

A sharp ring of a phone broke through the pack's easy chatter. Every male stopped talking and looked down the empty hallway toward the sound of the ringing. Bray gripped the arms of his chair, but didn't move.

Vixen took a deep breath. "If you'll all excuse me."

She didn't wait for anyone to respond. Not that any of them would have tried to stop her. Jackson stared at her steady retreat down the hallway.

"Bray?" Leighton asked.

"I don't know. If she wants us to know, she'll tell us." Bray shook his head. "Hey Foster, instead of running through the woods with Jackson tonight, you want to practice pouncing?"

Foster looked to his mom, who smiled and nodded.

"Yes, please."

"Hey, Foster, know what Vixen told me today?" Finley added another distraction to keep Foster from asking where Vixen went off to.

His eyes widened, and he shook his head. Vixen was one of his favorites of the pack and anything she said or did was gospel for him.

"She said she found us all Halloween costumes and we're going trick-or-treating this year." Finley spoke with a serious tone, as though he was sharing the secret of the universe with Foster.

"She did?" Foster asked for confirmation, along with all the others in the pack.

Finley nodded.

"Even us?" Allard gave Finley a look of accusation for not sharing sooner.

"All of us." Finley's smile split his face, it was so broad. "Even Bray and Vixen. But she wouldn't tell me the costumes she got. Just that they'll be here before Halloween and we were all participating."

Eleanor giggled and covered the noise with a sip of her drink.

"You know?" Jackson asked, leaning around Foster's back to get a better look at her blushing cheeks.

"She asked me my opinion."

Jackson's eyes narrowed. "Woman, just because you aren't lying doesn't mean we can't smell when it's a half truth."

Eleanor batted her eyelashes and feigned innocence. "Come on, Foster, let's get you cleaned up for wolf time."

Foster clamored over his chair, not even waiting to push it away from the table and raced back to his bedroom. Eleanor made him wash up and brush his teeth before wolf time. Not that he came back inside clean, but when Jackson tried to explain what a waste it was, she rolled her eyes and played the mom card. Jackson was weak when it came to the mom card. He could never find a satisfactory argument for it. Not even the dad card.

Eleanor followed him to verify Foster had washed his hands and brushed his teeth. Jackson figured she was also using it as an excuse to avoid an interrogation about their costumes.

"Bray." Vixen stood in the doorway to the kitchen. "Jackson, you too."

"What about Foster?" Jackson had mixed feelings about being involved in grown-up conversations. On one hand, he liked that Bray and Vixen were giving him more responsibility. On the other, more often than not the weight of the responsibility was a pain in his ass.

"Finley can go out with him if Foster's ready before we finish." Vixen tilted her head down the hallway to Bray and hers bedroom. "Let's go."

The walk down the hallway felt like a death march. Vixen's serious tone and Bray's silence settled an uneasy weight on Jackson's chest. Whatever they were going to talk about, Jackson wished he didn't have to be part of it. Bray closed the door behind them as they entered the bedroom.

A small bag, open but halfway packed with Vixen's clothes, sat on the bed. The bright yellow satellite phone that was her safety line to the outside world, sat next to the bag. She'd been on the phone while packing and once the call ended, came and got Jackson and Bray.

"Rip it off, Vixen." Jackson's mind went to the worst-case scenarios, all of them requiring sending Foster and Eleanor away to some place safer.

"Turns out Foster's classmates have big mouths."

"But it hasn't hit the news or we would have heard about it." Bray sat down on the bed and picked up the phone, his hands tightening around the hard plastic designed to survive the abuse of a war zone.

"As soon as the story leaked out, it got tamped down, but I'm not sure the story hitting the press would be worse. I need to make an appearance. Remind some people why they wanted me gone when they decided they no longer required my services. The colonel reached out because the news is causing a lot of interest from different agencies. Agencies we don't want asking questions."

"When do you have to leave?" Bray looked down at the phone in his hands.

"As soon as possible. Tonight. I won't be gone for more than a few days. Just show up, make a few non-threat threats, remind them they aren't safe and why they want to leave us alone."

"What does this mean for Foster?" Jackson worried for Vixen, but he worried about the safety of his son and his son's mother more.

"Nothing. They are both yours, which makes them mine. This news changes nothing." Vixen's eyes narrowed. "Are you hearing me, Jackson? This is the safest place they could be and I plan on keeping it that way. This. Changes. Nothing."

Bray closed his eyes and let out a long breath. "Jackson, it's now or never. Go to Eleanor. Let Finley and the others work with Foster's wolf tonight."

Jackson swallowed back his fear and gave both Vixen and Bray a quick nod before leaving them alone to say their goodbyes to another and heading down the hallway to find Eleanor. Bray was right. It was now or never. The time would never be perfect to convince Eleanor that they didn't need to limit themselves to being friends to co-parent a son. And instead of waiting for the right moment, Jackson needed to rip the band-aid off. At least if Eleanor rejected him, he wouldn't have to wonder about the what-ifs.

"Jackson?" Eleanor's whisper carried across the dark bedroom.

"Yeah." Jackson pushed off the door frame and took one step into the room. He'd been watching her sleep for several minutes after sniffing the air and finding her alone. Finley and the others must have convinced Foster's wolf to let him shift back and put him to bed in his own room.

He should have gone to her sooner, but like the coward he was, he sat in his room until well after Vixen left. Until well after the rest of the pack had gone to bed and fallen asleep.

Eleanor sat up in bed and patted the heavy comforter at the spot next to her legs. Jackson took another step into the room and closed the door behind him before crossing to the bed, but he didn't sit down.

"Is something wrong? Is Foster okay?"

Jackson's heart clenched at the worry in her voice. "No, he's fine. Everything's fine."

"Don't lie, Jackson. I might not sniff out a lie like you can, but I know when you aren't telling the truth."

"I swear. Foster's fine." Jackson sat down on the bed and hunched forward. Resting his elbows on his knees, he stared at the floor.

"So what has you so worried then?" Eleanor pressed her hand against Jackson's back and made small circles, like he'd seen her do with Foster when something upset him.

"You leaving. At dinner tonight, when we talked about Foster's growth spurt."

Eleanor sat further up and pressed her cheek against his shoulder. "Oh, Jackson. We aren't going anywhere. I mean, unless you want us to go. Is that why you're worried and Vixen and Bray pulled you away for a talk? They want me to leave?"

"No." Jackson shook his head. He was doing a piss-poor job of explaining things. "Everything feels temporary with you and Foster. Like you'll pull him away from me in a few weeks or months. Or even a few years from now. And then what will happen?"

"Jackson, for the first time in a long time, Foster is doing well. I mean, he's thriving here. I'll have to figure out school in about a year, but why would I take him away from the first place where he can be himself and doesn't have to lie about who or what he is?"

"But that's Foster. What about you, Eleanor? How are you ever going to be happy here? You're a human. And you were in school. You gave up a degree to bring Foster here."

"No. I made sure my son, our son, was safe. I didn't give up anything." Eleanor rubbed her nose against his shoulder blade. "And for what it's worth, if Foster wasn't reason enough to stick around, Mac dropped the mother-lode of original sources for my research. If Bray and Vixen made me leave, I'd just pack a bag, grab Foster's hand, march my way to Mac's front door, and convince him he needed to keep us around."

"That's fine for now. But what about later? When you realize what a bunch of screw ups, we are and Foster gets his wolf under control."

"Jackson."

"Yeah."

"Ask me."

"What am I supposed to ask you?"

"The question you're frightened of discovering the answer to."

"Will you stay? Here? With us? With me?"

"Yes."

"You mean it?" Jackson spun around to face Eleanor, cupping her cheeks between his hands and lifting her face so he could look into her eyes.

"I mean it. It would hurt Foster to leave here. And it would hurt me. And you too, I think. I don't want to hurt you." Eleanor covered Jackson's hands with her own and pressed her forehead against his, the way Vixen did with all the males in the pack. "I used to think Foster and I had the perfect family. I was wrong. Foster needs his father. Even if we haven't explained to him yet that you *are* his father."

"When he's ready. We'll both sit him down and explain it to him."

"When he's ready." Eleanor closed her eyes and smiled.

Jackson pressed his lips against hers. For a few moments she didn't do anything, just sat there. He wondered if he misread everything she said, but then her arms wrapped around his neck and she parted her lips for him and kissed Jackson right back. He pulled away, trailing light kisses across her jaw.

"Um Jackson?"

"Nope. No thinking. No questions. Just go with it. Because, woman, I don't think I can handle you saying you need to think about this right now." Jackson wrapped his arms around her and pulled her down on the bed. "We're just going to go ahead with this, you and me, and not worry about the what-ifs, since there aren't any what-ifs."

"There's a huge what-if. Foster is a what-if."

"Foster isn't a what-if." Jackson growled into her ear and pulled her back against his chest, wrapping his body around hers.

"He is if this doesn't work out. What happens if some sexy wolf shifter sashays her way into the pack and you feel some uncontrollable pull to her. What happens then? I can get over it. Eventually. But Foster won't."

"First, I love you seeming to think I'm not feeling that pull with you. Second, I hate you believing my feelings might be temporary."

"Oh, come on, I've heard the others talk about it. How they want to find their mates."

"Woman." Jackson's arms tightened around her waist and he tugged her until her ass pressed against his erection. No point in hiding what she did to him anymore. They had the conversation Vixen wanted, and now he just had to convince Eleanor that she was the one for him. "Vixen and Bray knew it before I did, but I'm pretty sure you're it for me."

"Pretty sure?"

"Woman!" Jackson growled and nuzzled his lips against the back of Eleanor's neck. "Sleep. Foster will come barreling in here before the sun cracks the horizon. We can argue about my feelings for you later."

"So this is how it is? You decide when and where we talk?" Eleanor wiggled against him, doing her best to pull away.

"No. But for tonight, yes. I just want to fall asleep with you in my arms and you knowing you're in my arms and why."

Eleanor turned and faced him. Her nose wrinkled and Jackson imagined her freckles disappearing in the crinkles. "You fall asleep with me in your arms?"

"Yes." Jackson kept his gaze on her. Even in the night's darkness, he knew she'd be able to see and hear the truth of his words. "At night. After Foster shifts back, I do too. My wolf gets enough time with you. He doesn't need to spend the night with you as well."

"We're going to discuss this later."

Jackson grinned and kissed the tip of her nose. "Not right now?"

Eleanor yawned and snuggled against him. "Nope. We're sleeping now."

"Woman." Jackson growled out and pressed his lips against the top of her head, tucking her closer to his body. "You undo me."

CHAPTER FOURTEEN

JACKSON wasn't avoiding Eleanor on purpose. After Vixen got that weird phone call then left in the middle of the night and everyone pretended they weren't nervous, Jackson spent most of his time in wolf form and in the woods. He still spent time with Foster, but wouldn't let the boy play in the woods like usual. And the others behaved strangely too and pretended they didn't hear Eleanor's questions.

The worst part wasn't that they kept Eleanor in the dark. Nope, the worst of it was the ungodly amount of testosterone and full-blown displays of dominance that resulted in constant bickering. Jackson wouldn't let any of the others get too close or spend too much time with either Eleanor or Foster without snarling and growling. And Bray wasn't any help either. Without Vixen there, his temper was short, and he was practically lost. It was like someone hid his favorite toy, revealed to him that Santa Claus and the Tooth Fairy didn't exist, and peed in his Cheerios all at the same time.

Eleanor was moments away from packing a bag and heading to Mac's with Foster until Vixen returned home. Thankfully, it didn't come to that. Vixen arrived later that day. She had only been gone two days and one night. Not even two full days since she left late at night, but it felt as though she'd been gone for a lifetime. Within minutes of walking through the door, everyone in the lodge settled down and the tension, once thick enough to cut with a knife, melted away.

Vixen didn't come home empty handed. She dropped several boxes on the table, and Eleanor knew exactly what they contained. The Halloween costumes. But Vixen wouldn't let anyone open the packages.

"Hey Foster?" Vixen called from across the table.

"Yeah, Vivi?" He started using Vivi after he heard Bray call her Vi. When Vixen didn't correct him, neither did Eleanor.

"Since tomorrow's Halloween and we have a big day planned, why don't we skip wolf time tonight? You and your mom can spend some quiet time together before bed, maybe?"

Foster looked between Jackson and Eleanor. The prospect of not having wolf time devastated her little boy, but he didn't want the others to see his disappointment.

"Can I join your quiet time?" Jackson asked Foster.

Foster considered the question, tilted his head to the side, and tapped his cheek in a close mimicry of Eleanor when she teased him by pretending to think about his request before inevitably giving him whatever it was he wanted. Eleanor bit down on the inside of her cheek and suppressed the laugh threatening to break free. Barely.

"I suppose, but we have to ask Mommy first."

"Of course," Eleanor wouldn't admit it, but she was relieved Jackson asked to be included because she hadn't wanted to be the one to invite him and ruin whatever had been planned.

"Jackson?" Bray's low grumble rolled across the room.

"I'm sure." Jackson stood behind Foster and lifted him high above the ground and over Jackson's head. "Some things are more important than others now."

"If you're certain."

"He is." Vixen ended the conversation before it turned into a cycle of two men saying the same thing over and over in an attempt to get the last word in. "All right then. Bray and I'll get the pizzas started and whenever anyone's hungry they can come in and graze."

Eleanor noted Vixen's tactic and filed it away for future use.

By the time Foster filled himself with enough pizza to cause Eleanor to worry about an upset stomach, quiet time ended as soon as it began. Foster read to both Eleanor and Jackson, but fell asleep in the middle of the book. Jackson slipped the book from Foster's hands and set it on the table next to the bed. Instead of scooping Foster up and returning him to his own bed to sleep, Jackson stretched out on Eleanor's bed then turned off the light.

Eleanor giggled. "Is this a family sleepover?"

"Yeah." Jackson wasn't nearly as amused as Eleanor.

"Okay, what's going on? Vixen's back, you don't have to keep me in the dark anymore." Eleanor whispered to keep from waking up Foster.

"Vixen's back. The pack needs to spend time with her, so they're all going out to shift and let their animals run."

Eleanor didn't know whether to be surprised by the admission itself or that she didn't have to pull it out of him. "Okay, why'd Vixen want to keep Foster inside then?"

"Because, Vixen isn't a wolf. She's... Well, I'm gonna tell you what she is, but you have to promise not to overreact."

"You realize that by virtue of telling me not to overreact, I probably will, right?"

"Yeah, but I'm hoping you'll stop and think before running away."

"Jackson…"

"Fine. Vixen's not a wolf, she's a griffin."

"Next you're going to tell me there are dragons and unicorns too."

"No." Jackson's forehead crinkled. "Well… no I don't think so, but a few months ago, I didn't think there were griffins either. Anyway, Vixen's griffin is sort of like Foster's wolf, except twenty times bigger and stronger and pretty much a killing machine. She wants Foster inside because we're not sure how her griffin will respond."

Okay. So there were a few ways to handle this news. Eleanor could either lose her ever-loving mind and run to Mac in a panic, which she considered a strong possibility. Or she could handle it like the researcher she was. If Foster hadn't suddenly turned into a wolf when he was a baby, Eleanor would have every reason to doubt any of Jackson's claims. But then again, if Foster hadn't suddenly turned into a wolf as a baby, she wouldn't have traveled halfway across the country and found herself living with a pack of wolf shifters. And a griffin shifter too.

"You're quiet." Jackson reached over Foster and pushed Eleanor's hair behind her ear.

"I'm processing."

Jackson closed an eye and peered at her. "Well what have you processed?"

Eleanor looked down at the top of Foster's head. "Is this news worth having a freak out over or do I save it for something bigger? Because, honestly, if you all have taught me anything in the past few weeks, it's there is always something bigger on the horizon that will make everything that has happened in my life so far seem mundane."

Jackson reached over Foster and cupped Eleanor's cheeks between his hands. "You're amazing."

"No. I'm a single human mother to a wolf shifter, I'm adaptable."

"Not a single mother anymore, Eleanor." A low protective rumble, that might have been a growl under different circumstances, came from Jackson. He pressed a kiss to Eleanor's forehead followed with a kiss to Foster's head.

"Jackson?"

"Hmm?"

"If Vixen needs to spend time with the pack, how come you aren't out there?"

"Because my mate and family will always come before the pack."

"Mate?"

"Woman, we had this conversation before. You are mine as much as Foster's mine. So, this right here? Us together as a family right now? It's worth a hundred nights running with the pack."

Eleanor closed her eyes and let out a long breath as Jackson slid his hand from her cheek to the back of her head.

"What's wrong, El? Besides everything else and you not believing you're my mate."

She dropped her hand and let her head fall to the pillow. "I wish Foster and I had something like wolf time."

"Woman, our son can't stop talking about you when you aren't around. You've heard how he talks about Vixen? Well, he mentions you a hundred times more." Jackson grinned at her. "You're his most favorite person and not even Finley bribing our son with bags of Cheetos and packages of Oreos will change that."

Eleanor curled up and tucked her hands under her head. "I like it when you called Foster our son."

"Yeah?"

"Uh huh."

Jackson ran his hand down her arm to her hand and laced his fingers through hers. "Go to sleep, El."

CHAPTER FIFTEEN

IT WOULD take a lot to convince the men that dressing up as the Village People was imperative to the success of their Halloween celebration for Foster, but Vixen was a master. She brushed off every excuse and even went as far as using the time and care she spent assigning each man a costume as an effective weapon in her guilt trip assault. In the end, Foster running around the front yard singing out his love for his white shoes at the top of his lungs convinced Jackson to put on his costume. He convinced the others to wear theirs as well because if he wore his, they sure as shit were wearing theirs. Vixen gave Jackson the Indian Chief costume and considering the costume, or lack of, the others had little ground to stand on in the complaint department.

From behind the closed door of her bedroom, Eleanor stared down at the costume Vixen had chosen for her. The tag said Sassy Snow

White, which Eleanor supposed was a step above Sexy Snow White. But between the blue velvet corset thingy that pushed Eleanor's boobs up and the heavy yellow satin skirt that flared out at the waist and showed off three quarters of her legs, it was impossible to misinterpret Vixen's intent. She'd even included a doozy of a pair of velvet slippers that had no business being worn outside. Vamp Snow White was a more appropriate name for the costume.

Eleanor might as well have been wearing a giant sign with the words: *Eat At Eleanor's. Psst, this is for you, Jackson, in case it's not obvious enough.*

Vixen hadn't considered the added complication of an almost four-year-old. If Jackson ever got brave enough to do more than kiss her, and she wasn't complaining about the kisses, Eleanor feared Foster would wander into the room and ask them what they were doing. Plus there was the whole mate thing.

Eleanor wasn't convinced Jackson's attraction to her was on the same plane as the connection between Bray and Vixen. Those two were in an entirely different stratosphere compared to every relationship Eleanor had witnessed from a distance. She had never seen such obvious devotion and when they were both in the same room, no one else existed. Eleanor didn't want to take away his opportunity to have that connection with someone. Sure, he was attractive, and he pushed all her buttons and to add to it Jackson was a great dad. And maybe, if she examined her body's reactions and the emotions simmering inside her, she'd admit one reason she wanted to stay at Broken Peak was because of Jackson. But she wasn't silly enough to believe lust meant love, not in the way the pack spoke about their future mates.

"Mommmmy!" Foster's cry of excitement carried all the way from the yard. "What's after brown?"

Before Eleanor could answer, Jackson shouted from the front of the lodge. "White!"

"Did you hear that, Mommy? Daddy Jackson knows my favorite song!"

Eleanor stopped lacing up the corset. Her fingers lost their ability to move independently of her hands and her arms fell to her sides.

Daddy Jackson.

They still hadn't sat down to explain to Foster who Jackson was to him. He must have figured it out on his own. Or maybe he overheard conversations he wasn't meant to.

Eleanor raced through putting on the rest of her costume, grabbed the pillowcase everyone had helped decorate to collect candy, hopped out the bedroom door while slipping on her shoes, raced through the hallway and out the front door just in time to see Jackson and Foster holding a stare off with one another.

Great.

To make matters worse, Vixen had assigned Jackson the costume with the least amount of coverage. They gave up any attempts at political correctness when they decided to cover his face with paint. Vixen even pulled up an image from Google to prove her point that without the face paint, the costume was just offensive. Eleanor wasn't certain it wasn't offensive regardless, but the face paint wasn't the worst of it.

Jackson stood in the middle of the yard in a leather loincloth, a pair of boots that might have been Uggs, a giant feathered headdress that hung down his back to the top of his very nice ass, and no shirt since the face paint extended down to his chest. It was all Eleanor could do not to stare at him.

"I'm supposed to carry this screwdriver around in my teeth?" Finley, dressed as a construction worker wearing too tight and too short jean shorts with a flannel shirt unbuttoned, but still tucked in, and the sleeves cut off, asked from the top step of the porch.

"Where'd you learn that name, Foster?" Jackson asked.

"Unca Finley. He also said you were a mother fu-"

Finley sprinted from the porch and pushed the screwdriver between Foster's teeth. "Haha, why don't you test this out for me, Foster? Then you can teach me how to hold it."

"Finley," Jackson growled low.

"What? It's true. Technically. Foster had to come from a mother, right, and since you're his dad, even though we've all been walking on eggshells not to mention it despite your kid being smart and already figuring it out. So, see, I did you all a favor."

Eleanor's jaw dropped. Jackson and she had decided they would sit Foster down and explain everything when they both agreed he was ready.

"Finley." Jackson growled low again, and Eleanor swore his hands clenched into fists to hide the flash of claws she thought she saw.

Foster pulled the screwdriver from his mouth. "Unca Finley, why is Daddy Jackson mad?"

"Heh, well see, kid..." Finley picked Foster up and tucked him under his arm. "I think it's time we collect the candy the Easter Bunny hid around the yard."

Foster let out a peal of laughter and squealed in delight. "Nooo. It's not Easter yet."

"It's not? Oh, then it must be time for Santa."

"Hehehehe nooooo. It's Halloweeeeeen!"

Finley might have crossed the parent boundary and shared something with Foster he had no right sharing, but there was no denying how good he was with Foster. The two spent almost as much time together as Jackson and Foster did. When Foster wasn't telling

Eleanor all about Jackson or Vixen, he was sharing stories about Finley.

As shitty as the situation was, and it was. Finley loved Foster and Foster adored Finley. Eleanor and Jackson would just have to figure it out. Besides, Foster didn't appear traumatized by the news. Jackson, on the other hand, had gone completely pale under the paint. He turned to Eleanor and grinned a goofy grin, as Vixen called it.

"He called me daddy."

"Well, we knew that was going to happen one of these days. Easier to rip the band-aid off then peel it back slow." Vixen stepped off the porch, hoisting the skirt of the blue short-sleeved and high-collared nightgown she was wearing above her ankles so she didn't trip. She wore her hair down except for a small bit she pulled back with a blue bow.

"Wendy?"

"Inside joke. The only reason Bray isn't wearing green tights is I had an easier time convincing him to dress like a cop, plus we needed six to pull off the entire look."

"Speaking of which..." Eleanor looked around the yard, but couldn't spot any of the others. It was easier to think about the rest of the pack dressing as The Village People then to consider the amount of therapy Foster was going to need to get over the fact Uncle Finley revealed the name of his father.

Bray placed his fingers to his mouth and released a shrill whistle, causing everyone except Eleanor to wince at the sound.

Jackson stumbled across the grass toward Eleanor. "Daddy?"

"Are you okay with that? We can tell him to call you something else."

"No. Yeah. I mean, no, he doesn't have to call me anything else. I think I kinda like it."

Leighton, Allard, and Tevin emerged from the front door, all of them glaring at Vixen while they fidgeted with their costumes.

Leighton tugged at the crotch of his jeans and scratched at his bare chest. "Really, Vixen, what made you think a cowboy would be a good choice for me?"

"The costume came with a holster, two guns, and a cowboy hat. I don't trust anyone else with guns."

"They're toy guns."

"Would you rather be a biker?"

Leighton had enough sense to keep quiet. Tevin did not.

"I don't think this is a biker costume, Vixen. It came with a mustache. And some kind of harness thingamajib, that I gotta tell you, is not at all comfortable. And how come Allard gets to wear a shirt that covers his chest?"

Allard lucked out in the Halloween costume lotto and dressed as the sailor. His chest might not have been bare, but the tightness of his pants bordered on being illegal according to decency laws.

All in all, Eleanor couldn't find much fault in Vixen's costume selections, except for her own. But before Eleanor could protest, Jackson wove his fingers through hers and tugged her along the path in Finley and Foster's wake.

"Come on, Mom."

Mom.

Eleanor liked the sound of it coming from Jackson's lips. She knew better than to believe she wouldn't be a complete wreck the first time Foster stopped calling her Mommy, but she'd deal with the despair if it meant Jackson continued calling her Mom. Not all the time, of course. But in moments like now, when he was about to experience trick-or-treating with his son for the first time, calling her Mom was perfect.

"Mommy! There are ghosts. Popa Mac made his path haunted!" Foster's squeal of joy hurried Jackson and Eleanor along the path.

"Careful of the…" Jackson looked down at Eleanor's shoes. "Woman, what in the name of these mountains are you wearing on your feet? That right there is worse than the getups Vixen has us wearing."

Without waiting for an explanation, Jackson scooped Eleanor up and swung her around to his back while following the sound of their giggling son down the pathway. He wove around the ghosts swinging from the higher branches of the trees.

"Mac really outdid himself." Eleanor giggled and batted away at the fake cobwebs strung from tree to tree. He'd even planted fake headstones and spooky skeletons along the pathway to give the woods an illusion of being haunted.

Foster might not have a normal childhood in the conventional sense, but everyone who lived around Broken Peak went out of their way to give Foster the best possible childhood. For a brief moment, Eleanor wondered if the lack of children his age would be a problem. Then Tevin and Allard sped past Jackson, hollering about how much candy they'd get and all her worries faded away. They all might have had twenty years on Foster, but it didn't stop them from playing around with him.

Eleanor tightened her arms around Jackson's chest and pressed her cheek against his shoulder with her nose buried in his neck. She took a deep breath through her nose and settled in for the ride to Mac's on Jackson's back. Jackson's scent, which was a blend of cut lumber, pine sap, flannel, and everything else that would fit in a bottle of cologne for a man who didn't need to wear cologne, comforted her, the same way smelling his scent on her sheets wrapped her up in a security blanket.

"Stop it." Jackson growled low.

"Stop what?" Eleanor lifted her head and pressed her chin down on the top of his shoulder.

"Sniffing me. It does things to you that then does things to me I can't act on."

Eleanor's eyes widened. Oh. Jackson shifted his hands, sliding them further up her thighs and pulled her tight against his back.

The problem with telling someone not to do something meant they almost always developed an insatiable need to do whatever it was they were told not to. Any parent understood that paradox. Jackson was going to learn it soon enough, but until then, Eleanor couldn't stop herself from pressing her nose against his neck and taking a deep breath.

She kept it up until Jackson didn't just grumble, he growled and his fingers tightened around her thighs. "Woman. If you don't stop, I'm going to miss my boy saying trick-or-treat to Mac."

"Why is that?" The sensations and emotions Eleanor attributed to lust ricocheted through her body.

"Because I'm about to go bushwhacking in more than one way."

Eleanor slapped her hand down on his shoulder. "Jackson."

"If you don't want to risk the chance of me losing my patience near a patch of poison ivy, then stop sniffing me."

"Mommy. Daddy Jackson. Hurry up!" Foster's impatient shout prevented Eleanor from testing whether Jackson would fulfill his promise.

"You heard your son, Jackson. Hurry up." Vixen came up alongside them with Bray as they all approached the group waiting for them in front of Mac's cottage.

Foster jumped up and down. "Can I go now? Huh? Can I?"

"Yes, yes, go ahead." Eleanor handed off the decorated pillowcase to Vixen who gave it to Foster.

They all sat back and watched Foster approach Mac's closed door. He peered at the door for several minutes before turning to face them. "There's no doorbell!"

"Knock, boy. Make a fist and pound on that door." Jackson slid Eleanor down his back to her feet, brought her to his side, and wrapped his arm around her shoulders, pulling her close to him.

"Oh!" Foster spun back around and followed Jackson's directions. Pounding his tiny fist against the wood.

"Who's out there making all that noise!" Mac opened the door and looked around the yard, deliberately not looking down.

"Me!" Jackson hopped up and down in front of Mac.

"Me? Who's me? I don't know any blue cats."

Foster laughed as though Mac told him the funniest joke ever. "It's me, Foster, Papa Mac!"

Mac bent forward and squinted his eyes, peering at Foster. "Why I don't believe it. You sure had me fooled."

"Psst!" Finley hissed out the sound to get Foster's attention, then nodded his head encouragingly.

"Oh yeah, I forgot." Foster grinned at Finley before turning back to Mac. "Trick-or-treat, smell my feet, give me something good to eat!"

"Finley!" Everyone shouted at Finley except for Tevin who was high-fiving him.

"I have to teach the boy things like that, If I'm going to be the favorite uncle." Finley didn't bother apologizing.

Vixen leaned in close to Eleanor and whispered, "You know at Christmas time we're going to hear about how Batman smells and Robin laid an egg."

Eleanor turned her head and hid her laughter against Jackson's chest.

"Look what I got, Mommy!" Foster came barreling down the path toward them, jumping up at the last minute.

Without missing a beat or looking away from Eleanor, Jackson caught Foster and hoisted him in the air before settling him on his hip opposite Eleanor. "Wha'cha get?"

"An entire bag of Snickers!"

"You were supposed to open the bag and give him a handful!" Vixen called out and rolled her eyes.

"There's plenty more." Mac shrugged unapologetically before returning inside his house and closing the door.

"Where to now!" Foster squirmed out of Jackson's arm and raced off to show Finley his first haul.

"Uncle Roose." Tevin tugged Foster's Pete the Cat hood back in place. "Lead the way."

After thirty minutes of walking back and forth from Mac and Roose's houses, Eleanor figured everyone would grow bored and want to go home. But the opposite happened. Everyone got into it. Vixen even convinced the boys to stand in front of Mac's door making the letters YMCA with their arms with Bray and Jackson posed on the ends with their arms crossed over their chests.

"Tell me you got a picture of that." Eleanor spoke under her breath just as a flash came from the side of Mac's house.

"Roped Roose into helping." Vixen grinned at Eleanor. "And now we have our family Christmas picture. We'll have to do a girls' pose and a few of just Foster and one of all of us not in costumes."

Eleanor stumbled back a few steps with Vixen's words. *Family Christmas picture.* She supposed that's what they were. A family. In her mind, the family was Eleanor, Foster, and Jackson. But to Vixen, and all the others, they were all one big family.

She closed her eyes and took a deep breath as a pair of muscular arms wrapped around her and pulled her tight against a bare chest.

"El? What's wrong? Are you okay?" Jackson tucked her head under his chin and held her close.

"She's fine. She just had one of those epiphanies that will sneak up and kick you in the ass if you aren't careful." Vixen squeezed her shoulder before walking away and leaving the two of them alone together. "What did papa Mac give you this time, Foster?"

"What happened?" Jackson leaned back and peered down at her.

"Nothing. Really. Vixen mentioned something is all."

Jackson's eyes glowed brightly for a moment before fading. "What did she say?"

"Something about family." Eleanor tilted her head back so she could look Jackson in his eyes. "She broadened my definition."

The corners of Jackson's lips lifted in a slight smile as he bent down and kissed the tip of her nose. "Good. It's about time you figured that out. Now we just need to convince you that *both* you and Foster are mine."

CHAPTER SIXTEEN

VIXEN and Bray kept to themselves while Foster and the rest of Jackson's packmates divvied up the candy. The two Alphas sat in a quiet corner with their heads bent together. Despite all appearances they weren't talking aloud with each other, Jackson had no doubts they were doing that silent communication thing.

Whatever happened in DC, Vixen had kept it to herself. Jackson expected her to call him aside like she had done the other night, instead she plastered on a smile for Foster's sake and kept her emotions from leaking out to the rest of the pack.

The leaking thing was another one of Vixen's little tricks they learned about after her griffin made its first appearance. Apparently, the griffin was capable of impressing Vixen's emotions on others and even going so far as to amplify them. It explained why complete strangers trusted her and her enemies held an intense hatred and fear of her. Great to use against threats, but sometimes dangerous for friends and packmates. Mac had been working with her, trying to use the griffin to help focus the emotions like a futuristic weapon or super power from a movie. The lessons hadn't gone as well as they hoped, and Mac shifted the priority from focusing the emotions to tamping down the unintended emotion leakage.

The entire evening was perfect. Foster ran from Roose to Mac's house non-stop and never grew bored with knocking on the same two doors all night. Roose and Mac got into the fun and added costume changes to their repertoire later in the evening. Foster had whispered to Jackson that he knew it was Papa Mac behind the mask, but he was pretending he didn't because Papa Mac got so happy when he thought he fooled Foster.

And now four adult male wolf shifters sat in a circle with a pup and stared down at the mountain of candy Foster collected. One gorgeous human woman watched with a nervous eye as Foster stuck what was probably the twenty-third piece of candy into his mouth. And Jackson was torn between the blissful ignorance of not knowing how Vixen's meeting went and the urge to learn everything so he could keep both Eleanor and Foster safe.

A sugar coma hit Foster like a freight train. One minute he was bouncing in place and chattering away a mile a minute, and the next his chin dipped and his eyelids drooped closed despite the kid's best efforts to keep his eyes open. Jackson pushed off the chair, ready to carry Foster to bed, but Finley beat him to it.

"I got this. You take care of what you need to." Finley lifted his chin in Bray and Vixen's direction.

Finley spoke quietly enough, but Eleanor picked up enough words and narrowed her shrewd gaze on Jackson. He knew that look. A conversation was coming.

"Make sure you wake him up to brush his teeth before you put him to bed, Finley." Eleanor stopped him and kissed the top of Foster's head. "And make sure he pees too. And wash his face."

Finley blew a raspberry at Eleanor. "How am I supposed to be fun uncle Finley if I make him do all the not fun things?"

"Because fun uncle Finley doesn't want mean daddy beating the shit out of him for not listening to nice mommy's directions." Jackson crossed his arms over his chest and stared at the back of Finley's head, reinforcing his words with a small dominant push.

Eleanor lifted her gaze from Finley to Jackson and her smile went all sweet. Jackson crossed the room to her and pulled her into his arms as Finley carried Foster down the hallway. When she settled her weight against him, he pulled her down into the chair with him and settled her on his lap. The others noted the display of affection but said nothing. There was still candy to claim.

Jackson rubbed his cheek against the back of her head and let out a soft sigh of contentment.

"What's happening, Jackson?" Eleanor leaned back against his chest. "Or is this one of those, we'll talk about it later moments? Because if it is? Well, you should know, later is fast approaching."

He closed his eyes, and the words poured from his mouth. "Honestly, El, Vixen left to take care of a potential problem, but she hasn't said anything to me about what happened. And if she told Bray, he's not saying anything."

When he finished, he opened his eyes, expecting Eleanor to be giving him that look of disappointment she used on Foster to guilt him into behaving. Instead, she stared across the room at the pile of candy. Eleanor took a deep breath, pushing her breasts up and out. Both Jackson and his wolf growled. The pack didn't realize it, but between them and Foster, they had achieved expert levels of cock blocking.

Jackson shifted Eleanor in his lap, needing to ease the pressure of her perfect ass on his growing erection. He hadn't changed out of the costume Vixen gave him to wear, except to remove the headdress, and the loincloth wasn't helping the growing matter. While living in a pack demanded a lowering of inhibitions and modesty because shifting while still wearing clothes was a pain in the ass, claiming one's mate in public wasn't encouraged. Stripping naked and standing around outside, perfectly fine. Fucking in public, not so fine. Some kinds of shifters enjoyed public claimings, but wolves didn't and since Vixen was the only griffin they knew, Jackson assumed griffins didn't either. Her claiming might have been semi public, but the fun parts that usually accompanied claimings always happened behind closed doors. Or at least when no one was around to watch them.

Vixen swiveled her head in that odd raptor like way of hers and stared at Jackson and Eleanor. Though Vixen and Bray were clear across the room and out of hearing distance for as softly as Eleanor and Jackson were speaking, even with sensitive shifter hearing, Vixen heard every word they said.

"Boys, clean up the candy and bring it to the kitchen." Vixen dismissed the pack.

Eleanor slid from his lap, but Jackson pulled her back. "Not us. Just them."

"But…" Eleanor twisted around to face him, rubbing in the worst places.

Jackson groaned and dug his fingers into her hips to stop her movements. Stopping her wouldn't get rid of his hard-on, only a cold shower would succeed, but he didn't want things getting worse. "Trust me. Vixen wants us to stay and you don't want to have her say it right now."

"Is she angry?" Eleanor whispered.

"No. She's doing her Alpha thing, and she doesn't have as fine of control over it as Bray."

Eleanor watched the others gather armfuls of candy and retreat to the safety of the kitchen. She looked as though she wanted to follow them and Jackson didn't blame her.

When they no longer heard Allard and Tevin arguing about who got the Twix bars, Vixen cleared her throat. Both Jackson and Eleanor snapped their heads in Vixen and Bray's direction. Vixen tilted her head toward the large couch and Jackson didn't protest the silent command. He stood with Eleanor in his arms and carried her to the couch where he sat down and settled her right back in his lap, even though there was plenty of room for her to sit next to him.

Vixen opened her mouth, but no words came out. For the first time since ever, the female Alpha was speechless. Jackson looked at Bray and lifted his eyebrows in a silent question. Bray gave a small shake of his head. He was going to let Vixen handle it. Jackson prepared himself for the worst news and wished he could have warned Eleanor. She tended to do better when he helped manage her expectations by giving her an idea of where the news fit on the emotion spectrum.

"It turns out that Foster's classmates are better at talking than we thought. It also turns out that some government agencies are better at suppressing stories than I believed possible." The words poured out of Vixen's mouth.

Jackson tightened his arms around Eleanor's waist before she could leap to her feet. She fell back with a grunt, but didn't give up her attempts to free herself. Eleanor enjoyed pacing when she wanted to think. Foster taught Jackson that. The first time Eleanor stalked the length of the room, Foster tugged on Jackson's hand and told him to nod his head and say yes and it would be fine. The kid might only be close to four, but he was wise in the ways of his mother. Somehow, Jackson didn't think Vixen would appreciate Eleanor's pacing.

"Vi's taken care of it. We don't have anything to worry about right now." Bray cleared his throat and leaned forward on his knees.

"What do you mean she's taken care of it?" Eleanor wriggled in Jackson's lap and tugged at his forearms, but he wasn't budging. "Foster's not yet four, his classmates either just turned four or are younger than him."

Vixen rolled her eyes. "Please. I didn't take care of things that way, though it would have been easier to relocate the families. We-"

"We? Who's we?" Eleanor asked another question and Jackson waited for Vixen to explode.

The explosion never arrived, surprising both Jackson and Bray from Bray's wide eyes and dropped jaw.

"Some friends. Well, not friends, more of a friend and an ally. They're helping and will keep an eye out. If anything changes, they'll tell me. But for now, we're just going to sit tight. Except you and Foster can't go into town."

"We haven't gone into town."

"And you won't be going now," Vixen smiled and leaned back in her chair. "See nothing's changed."

Vixen's smile was too self-satisfied for Jackson's taste, but he wasn't brave or stupid enough to challenge her.

"We don't expect any problems, but we're going to take precautions like running patrols at night." Bray leveled his gaze on Jackson. "Tonight, that's you and me. Tomorrow, Vi is taking Leighton out."

Jackson turned Eleanor to the side and pulled her into his lap. The pieces weren't fitting together and he couldn't figure out the end game. Vixen always had an end game. Bray had just hoped they got to the end, but Vixen taught them all that sometimes the journey wasn't nearly as important as the destination. Jackson got the feeling now was one of those times.

"Why are you telling the others this?" Eleanor flipped her gaze between Bray and Vixen, asking the question Jackson wanted answered.

"Because Bray's giving Jackson a crash course on leading a two-man patrol. For the next week or two, Jackson, Bray, or I will lead the patrols. He's not going to have much time for Foster, or you, until we're satisfied my message was received loud and clear."

"I can see why you'd be concerned about Foster, but I don't understand why you're worried about me."

Bray snorted, and Jackson let out a soft growl.

Vixen laughed. It wasn't a polite laugh either, it was the kind that came from her stomach and caused tears to fall from her eyes. "You still haven't accepted it yet? Never mind, you will. And when you do, you'll have an uncontrollable urge to spend as much time with Jackson as possible. When that doesn't happen because he has responsibilities to the pack, you'll get angry, but won't understand why. And then you'll remember this conversation and instead of being angry with Jackson, you'll be pissed with me."

Bray lifted his gaze to Eleanor and gave her a small smile, "we're working on her tact."

Jackson almost told Bray they needed to work a lot harder. Almost. Jackson hadn't gotten any more stupid or brave in the past several minutes.

"I don't understand." Eleanor twisted in Jackson's lap, much to his chagrin, and peered at Vixen.

"Alphas?" Jackson coughed and cleared his throat.

"Of course," Bray took Vixen's hand and stood, bringing her with him as he headed out of the room and down the hall. "Come on, let's leave them alone for a bit. We can pick out the Baby Ruths."

"Jackson?" Eleanor spun in his lap to face him, straddling his thighs to better see his eyes.

"Vixen's worried someone might think we're weak and try to attack us again."

"Again?"

"When Vixen first arrived here, she was being hunted by a government agency. They sent a team in to eliminate her, but it didn't go as planned and it was a mess. The helicopter exploding, the griffin disemboweling someone; it took a long time to clean up the mess."

"Disemboweling?" She stared at him as if he grew a third and fourth head.

"It was bad, and it was bad because they sneaked up on us. Vixen warned Bray that they'd come after her. We believed her, but we never thought they'd sent a team in. This is Vixen planning for the end game."

"And what's the end game?"

"Keeping us safe. And keeping our secret a secret."

"Jackson, maybe Foster and I should go somewhere else. If they know we're here..."

In response to her suggestion, Jackson stood and scooped up Eleanor before she could begin her pacing thing. "You two are not going anywhere. You two are staying right here. Make no mistake, El, you run off, and I will spend the rest of my life looking for you. And when I find you, I'll watch from a distance until you allow me closer."

"Humans call that stalking." Eleanor's words weren't chastising, instead they bordered on teasing.

"Yeah, so do shifters, but I'll keep my distance and won't cross the line to creepy stalker." Jackson strode past her bedroom door and Fosters.

"Jackson?"

"Hmm?"

"Where are we going?"

"Our room."

"Our?" She twisted in his arms and looked over his shoulder. "You just passed my room."

"Nope. Not anymore. Wolves move fast, Eleanor. We can't help it." He pushed into his bedroom and kicked the door closed. "I don't care if I've claimed you or not. You and Foster are mine and you're going to stay with me. I can keep you safe. I *will* keep you safe. And tonight, I need you to sleep here. In my bed while I'm out or I am going to spend my patrol duty worrying about you."

He dropped her on the bed before she protested, then grabbed a change of clothes from his dresser. He needed to dress before going out on patrol. Jackson turned as he was pulling up the black fatigue pants and zipping them up, prepared to face Eleanor coming up with reasons why she should spend the night in her bedroom. Instead, he found Eleanor staring at his hands.

Or more exactly, the location of his hands.

Sweet Eleanor, who blushed whenever the pack stripped for wolf time with Foster, had a flush to her cheeks, but it wasn't from embarrassment.

Jackson recognized the look on her face. He'd witnessed Vixen look at Bray the same way and Jackson was sure he stared at Eleanor with that same expression countless times before.

He slipped on the long-sleeved t-shirt and coughed, "Eleanor?"

She lifted her gaze, but looked away from him, "yeah?"

"You'll be here when I come back." It wasn't a question, but Jackson wouldn't consider it a command either.

"Yeah," Eleanor looked down at her hands in her lap, "but Jackson, we're having a conversation, one where both of us talk, when you get back."

"Thank you," Jackson nodded and smiled at her. Before he chickened out, he crossed the room in four long strides and pressed his lips against the top of her head then turned and hurried from the room.

Eleanor called from his bedroom as he closed the door, "Jackson, be safe. Please."

Jackson grinned like a fool as he strode through the hallway back to the front of the lodge and to the porch. Bray already waited for him, dressed in similar clothing.

"All good?" Bray handed Jackson a Glock and a belt with a knife.

"Yeah. All good."

CHAPTER SEVENTEEN

"HOW'D she take it?" Bray asked. Jackson crouched as he studied the soft ground close to the river for prints. He looked up at Bray and lifted his shoulders. "Not sure yet. We're having a conversation. Whatever that means." He lifted his chin and sniffed the air. "This feels wrong."

The way Vixen explained it, patrolling was just a precautionary measure. She told him and Eleanor she'd taken care of the reason for the call. Except the air in the woods was silent. Too silent.

"She's got a good head on her shoulders. Plus, she kept your boy a secret for four years and raised him alone. She'll be fine. While you're doing your conversating, remember she's strong, like Vi but in a different way." Bray snapped a picture of what might have been a footprint or a mark from a rock or branch that disturbed the ground. "Let's keep going."

A low rumble came from Jackson, but he followed Bray's order and ignored his wolf pushing for release. The last thing Bray, or the rest of the pack needed was Jackson's wolf charging through the woods because he thought there was a threat. With Eleanor and Foster back at the lodge, his wolf ached for the release to run, but the beast would go after anything. Hell, even Mac and Roose wouldn't be safe from his wolf.

As they followed the deer trail, Jackson pulled his gun free from his belt. Just because neither man nor wolf could identify what was wrong didn't mean nothing was wrong. Bray had done the same. As long as they walked the woods, Jackson didn't have to talk about Eleanor and Bray didn't have to hear how the organized patrolling felt unnatural. On instinct, when they shifted, their wolf might spend time at the borders of their territory. And sometimes, as men, they walked along the edges of their territory. But they'd never organized the patrols. Instead, they listened to the wants of their wolves.

Eleanor had to be the reason for Jackson's discomfort. He left her alone after unequivocally stating she was his. In most packs, once one side of a pairing declared his or her intent and the other side accepted, the newly mated couple spent days alone together before venturing out for necessities like food. Jackson accepted he and Eleanor wouldn't have a prolonged mating, not with Foster in the same house, but a night would have been nice. And with Foster in a sugar coma, it was a perfect night for a claiming and mating. Of course, all that assumed Eleanor would accept the claiming.

Jackson growled low.

Bray came to an abrupt halt and glared over his shoulder at Jackson. "Think you can keep from growling every forty-five seconds?"

"What if she says no?"

"She won't. She might at first, but she won't." Bray rolled his eyes before looking forward and resuming his steady stride through the woods. "Concentrate on our task instead of letting your mind consider all the hypotheticals."

Keeping his eyes closed, Jackson let out a long breath. Bray was right. Thinking about Eleanor wouldn't make the patrol go any faster and would only distract him. He needed to finish patrolling for the night, head back to the lodge and Eleanor, and then instead of his mind wandering off with ideas of their mating, he'd have to convince her they needed to take advantage of the moment before Foster woke up in the morning.

Bray's arm came up, and he made a fist. A signal Vixen had taught them all. Stop. Don't move, don't ask questions, and don't make any noise until the arm came back down. They were a few feet from a clearing and the thick trunks of the trees hid them in the shadows.

A gust of wind blew and the heavy evening clouds floated in front of the moon, dulling its bright light for a moment and revealing a green glow from the clearing before returning to its full glow and lighting up the woods.

Jackson's wolf urged him to shift and race back to his mate and pup. A mate who hadn't yet agreed to be his mate, but his wolf didn't care about technicalities. He pushed his wolf back and crept forward on slow, silent steps until he stood next to Bray.

Three men stood in the middle of the clearing with their heads bent together looking down at the source of the green light. Jackson and Bray dropped to the ground and peered through the cover provided by the bushes and roots.

The trespassers didn't look up once from the screen. Stupid humans. Jackson and Bray might have been quiet, but they weren't silent. And they weren't even downwind. All the human men had to do was pay more attention to their surroundings than the screen and they would have noticed they were no longer alone in the woods.

Jackson pressed his shoulder against Bray's and circled his head around the clearing towards the other side. Bray delivered a curt nod and crept forward, closer to the edge of the cover. Jackson slipped further back into the woods. With one careful foot in front of the other, he made his way around the perimeter of the clearing. Once he found a spot to watch the men without being seen, he crouched down and allowed his wolf to come forward enough for his eyes to shift. Bray saw the signal and returned it. Any human would just notice the eyes of some animal reflecting in the moonlight. Not an ideal way to communicate, but it was perfect for keeping noises that human ears could pick up to a minimum.

"Damn it, this is a suicide mission and you know it."

"If she's here, there's no way we succeed. You heard what happened to the last team."

"The last team was a wet team. They came in to eliminate, we're here to extract. Different mission."

"She won't see it that way, and we're going to end up exactly like the last team."

"All we have to do is get the kid and get the hell out of here. We don't even have to break in. Just find a spot to hunker down, then when the kid comes out to play during the day, we snatch him. By the time they figure out he's gone and not just being a kid, we'll be long gone."

"And Vixen will hunt down our asses." The man threw his hands up in the air and stepped away from the other two. "I didn't sign up for this shit. No kids. She taught us all that. Never kids and no innocents. This kid is an innocent. Hell, she's an innocent if we use her standards and not the agency's."

What the hell?

Was this the off feeling? Some strangers came into their woods, their land, intent on kidnapping a child?

Jackson swallowed down the growl threatening to break free while pushing his wolf back. The wolf wanted to eviscerate all three men, even the two who appeared to be against the fucked up mission. Knowing Bray, he was fighting the same battle with his wolf. Vixen could take care of herself and then some, but it wouldn't matter to Bray's wolf. Men, armed men, threatened Bray's mate and Jackson's son. The wolves wanted them dead. Jackson wanted them dead too, and he figured so did Bray.

The problem with separating from each other and not having a clear way of communicating reared its ugly head. Jackson couldn't say for sure what Bray was going to do or what Bray wanted Jackson to do. Jackson slipped back into the woods and began stripping off his clothes. If his wolf wanted free, Jackson would give him his freedom. He grabbed the back collar of his shirt and pulled it up over his head when Vixen's voice called out to him in his mind. Not her literal voice and not even her words, but they might as well have been.

You have the advantage. The moment you act, you lose the advantage. Stay hidden and listen, you'll learn more.

Jackson didn't think the words came from his wolf either, since he let out a loud growl in Jackson's mind as soon as he dropped his shirt, crouched down, and crept forward to do exactly as the voice suggested.

The man who stepped away let the other two argue.

"We're dead men if we go back empty handed and we're dead men if we go through with the plan."

"So what do you suggest? Fall off the grid like her? That didn't exactly end well."

"She's still alive."

"And now she's vulnerable because she has a family we can exploit."

"Are you insane? It's a fucking kid and we aren't fucking exploiting that." The second of the two men who had concerns about the morality of their mission stepped away. "You do whatever the hell you want, Church, but me and Emerson are getting the fuck out of here."

Well, at least Jackson had two of the three men's names. Not that it made a difference.

Emerson and the unnamed man walked away, giving their backs to Church. Jackson smirked. Vixen would have had their hides for giving their backs to an unknown variable. Church might have been a team-mate, or even a friend, but as soon as they disagreed about the mission, he became an unknown.

Jackson caught the flash of gold moving through the woods after the retreating men. Bray was following those two. That left Church for Jackson's wolf. Jackson grinned and so did his wolf. He might not get all three of the men, but at least he'd get one.

Church bent his head over the screen. Probably trying to find the best hiding place to snatch Foster. Keeping his eye on Church, Jackson took a few steps back and pulled off his clothes as quietly as possible. Not that he had to worry.

Church was too preoccupied by the information on the screen to pay attention to the surrounding woods. He didn't notice the change that came over the woods when Jackson let his wolf out. He didn't notice the gigantic wolf stalking up to his back. But he sure as hell noticed when the wolf pounced on him from behind and clamped his jaws around Church's neck.

Jackson's wolf wasn't as quick a killer as Vixen's griffin, but his wolf was efficient. The power in the wolf's jaws crushed down on the man's larynx while the long canines tore through the jugular. Less than thirty seconds passed from pounce to Church's last breath. It wasn't a painless death, but it was quiet and fast.

The wolf didn't bother with the still-warm body. He wanted the other two. Even if they hadn't outright threatened the pup, they represented the threat, and it was enough for the wolf. Jackson pulled the wolf back, bit by little bit until the beast surrendered his body back to the man.

He didn't bother looking at the dead man or even stripping him of his gear. Jackson went back to the woods and pulled on his clothes. Running through the woods naked wasn't on anyone's list of fun activities, unless it was coed naked running through the woods and someone had cleared out the branches and trimmed back the bushes ahead of time. Once dressed, Jackson returned to the body. As much as he wanted to leave it for the scavengers and critters who made these woods their home, Vixen wouldn't be happy and Bray would make Jackson go back to clean up the body.

Stripping off the weapons, Jackson added them to his belts and pockets. The electronic gear, he broke. Anything that might provide a simple way to track a location got crushed into tiny pieces, carried to the river, and thrown into the water.

Twenty minutes later, Jackson was hiking through the woods, holding on to the dead body by an ankle, and dragging it behind him. Sure, he could have taken care not to step over every protruding root or walking close to the bushes with their needle-sharp branches. But he didn't. Church was going to take Jackson's son. Just steal the pup away from his mom. Church deserved everything his corpse got. And Jackson's wolf agreed wholeheartedly if the wagging tail was anything to go by.

"Vixen's going to be pissed when she learns you're here."

Bray's voice carried back to Jackson, and he hurried his pace. He needed to drop the body off and get back to the lodge to check on Foster.

"We know why you're here, which was your first mistake. Vi's got a soft spot for that kid, soft enough to dress herself up in a Halloween costume for his benefit. So, why don't we skip the bravado and fast forward to the part where you tell me who sent you and maybe I can convince her to make your death painless."

Jackson broke through the woods and heaved the dead body at the bound men's feet. Somehow, Bray had overwhelmed the two men, disarmed them, and tied their arms behind them and around a tree, and also tied their feet together. No way the men could escape with Bray, and now Jackson, watching.

"His death wasn't painless. Quick. But not painless."

"We were leaving," one of the men, Emerson maybe, pleaded.

"Yeah, but you still came here." Bray crossed his arms over his chest and stared down at the men.

"We didn't know our target. That's how it works. They tell only one of us the details. Then once we get here, the mission is revealed. We didn't know what we were walking into until Church," the man looked down then away from the dead body, "told us. There's a reason they gave the details to Church and not us. They knew we'd balk."

"Who sent you?" Jackson narrowed his eyes, but let his wolf come forward.

The bound men jerked back at the sight of Jackson's glowing eyes and he grinned at them. Sometimes it paid to let the wolf come forward enough for the animal to show beneath the skin of the man.

The man looked at Emerson, who nodded once.

"Best guess is the man whose office she broke into then told to fuck off."

"And who's that?" Bray leaned back against a tree trunk, appearing bored.

"The President."

Oh shit. No wonder Vixen hadn't gone into any details of her meeting. And just who the hell was Vixen in her past life that she could break into the Oval Office?

Emerson stared at Jackson, "you didn't know."

Jackson closed his eyes for a few seconds and let out a long breath.

The end game had changed.

CHAPTER EIGHTEEN

ELEANOR had tried to stay awake, but the combination of nerves and excitement from spending the evening with the pack trick-or-treating pushed her into an exhaustion that welcomed sleep when her head hit Jackson's pillow. It hadn't been a sound slumber though. Similar to the nights before coming to Broken Peak when Foster was sick or shifted, Eleanor hovered at the point between sleep and wakefulness.

When she sat straight up in bed with the heavy comforter pressed against her chest, it wasn't from the cries of a sick child or the fearful shrieks her son struggling through the shift from boy to wolf. She couldn't see anything, but she knew Jackson was there. Like she knew he was there the night Vixen had left the lodge.

"Jackson?"

"Yeah." His voice sounded different from the man she had grown close to. He was careful to keep his wolf separate. She understood from spending time with the others and from Foster, that the animal was always close by, biding his time inside the man until the man let him free.

She took a deep breath through her nose and his familiar masculine scent invaded her senses. He might not sound like Jackson, but there was no mistaking his scent. It enveloped her in a blanket of security.

"What happened? Are you hurt? I thought you were supposed to spend the night patrolling."

"The end game changed, I'm not hurt, and things happened that made Bray and me decide to come back home."

She didn't hide her smile as he answered her questions in the order she asked them. Not that she liked his answers, but there were some habits of his that amused her. His need to answer things in the order asked was top of the list. She considered inviting him to his own bed, but something was riling him up or he would have crawled under the covers with her instead of lurking in the corner of his room.

Eleanor slipped out of bed, crossed the floor to Jackson, and took his hand in hers. "Come on. I'll get a shower started and you can clean up." She tugged his reluctant body across the room to the bathroom.

Flipping on the light in the bathroom, she left Jackson standing in the door and turned on the shower for him. She learned that while the lodge had plenty of hot water, it sometimes took a while to heat the pipes that led to the showers. She tugged the curtain closed to keep both the water and steam from escaping into the bathroom and turned to face him.

He stared at her just above her knees and rocked from side to side. "Jackson?"

He refused to lift his gaze.

"Jackson." She used her mom voice, the one used with Foster when he wouldn't pay attention to her. And what do you know? Jackson's head snapped up and his gaze locked on her eyes.

It took all her self-control not to step back from the intensity of his stare. The man standing in front of her was nothing like the man she had spent time with. His grizzled voice matched his expression. His already sharp cheek bones were even more pronounced. The square lines of his jaw were even more angled. The sharp points of his elongated canines pressed down against his bottom lip. And his eyes glowed with a steady pale green light instead of the brief flashes when his wolf approved of whatever it was she was doing.

Both man and wolf were fighting something, but not against each other. Eleanor didn't understand it or how she came to the realization, but both wolf and man were in lockstep together and that was why they seemed to share the same space.

Jackson snarled and took a step closer to her.

"Get in the shower," Eleanor stepped to the side and pulled back the shower curtain. Jackson's appearance frightened her. Not because Jackson scared her, but because of whatever was out there caused man and wolf to meld together.

He pulled his shirt over his head and dropped it to the floor while toeing his boots off. His pants came off next, and as much as Eleanor wanted to take every inch of him in, now wasn't the time. He stood in front of her strong and proud, she imagined he was strong and proud in every way, but didn't drop her gaze from his face to confirm it.

"Get in," she lowered her voice to a near whisper even though there was no one else in the room to hear her words. As soon as Jackson stepped into the shower, she pulled the curtain closed. Eleanor released a long breath she didn't realize she was holding. "I'll get you something to change into."

Eleanor bent over and picked up his discarded clothing and boots before leaving the bathroom. She needed to get out of the bathroom before she climbed in the shower with him and did all sorts of things that would be inappropriate considering something bad enough had happened for Bray to call off the patrol early.

She just needed something to do, to keep busy while Jackson finished his shower. Then, once both man and wolf had calmed down enough, she'd convince him to get in bed with her. Once she got his defenses down enough, she could get the entire story out of him, but until then, she didn't need to be thinking about the way his mere presence sent a wave of warmth through her or caused her body to tingle in places that usually required help from a battery operated friend to achieve tingling.

The water shut off, and she was still standing in front of Jackson's dresser. She hadn't even tossed his worn clothes into the hamper. Cripes, how long had she been standing there doing nothing?

"El?"

Jackson's voice was still wild and full with the rough rasp, and it wreaked havoc on her nerve endings, sending messages of want and need to the rest of her body and her brain. She pressed her hands against the top of the dresser to keep from falling over and turned her head toward the bathroom. His massive form took up the space of the doorway, blocking the light from the bathroom and creating a halo of illumination behind him. He had wrapped the towel loosely around his waist. Eleanor was grateful the shadows hid most of his body from her view.

God. What was wrong with her? Sure, she appreciated the aesthetics of an attractive male, but she had never experienced the urge to climb a man like a tree. Of course, she hadn't met a man as large as a tree before either.

She pushed off the dresser and used the momentum to propel her across the floor toward him. Jackson's palms pressed against the doorway as his stare followed her approach. His entire body shook with the tension of a tightly strung bow. When she stood toe to toe with him, Eleanor looked up at his face, refusing to look away from his hungry gaze that penetrated all reason and logic to target emotion.

Jackson's chest rose and fell with deep breaths and she watched in fascination the way his muscles undulated beneath his skin. She pressed her hands against the pectorals of his chest, spreading her fingers wide. When he still didn't move, she slipped her hands across his chest and down his sides then wrapped her arms around his waist and pressed her cheek against his chest. Jackson remained still for a few minutes more before bringing his arms down and embracing her against him.

The towel hid nothing, not that there was much in the way of clothing that could hide the size of Jackson's erection, but the towel was the least effective. Jackson gripped the back of her shirt and pressed his hips forward.

"My shirt." He wasn't asking her as much as speaking his thoughts aloud.

"After you left, I guess it was easier to stay here instead of going back to my room to change."

"I like it. You in my clothing." His gruff and growling voice was back. It wasn't just Jackson who enjoyed Eleanor wearing his clothes, the wolf seemed to take pride in it as well.

"I was being lazy."

"I don't care. In fact, I think we should just get rid of all your clothes and you can wear mine from now on." His arms tightened around her shoulders, pulling her body tight against his.

Since she wasn't very tall to begin with and Jackson was a veritable giant, the top of her head hit right between his pecs and his erection hit right at her belly. His body shuddered with the contact and she pressed closer.

"El, I won't claim you until you're ready, but I am seconds from claiming you in other ways. If you don't want that to happen, you need to say so right now. I don't think I'll be able to stop in another second."

Eleanor didn't answer. She pushed up to her toes and kissed her way up his chest as far as she could reach. Jackson, or his wolf, growled low, and the rumble vibrated against her causing a new flood of tingles to rampage through her body. He slid his hands down her sides to the back of her thighs and hoisted her up his body. She wrapped her legs around his waist and continued to let her lips explore the muscled planes of his chest and collarbone.

Jackson carried her to the bed, lowering her down onto the mattress so his body covered hers. Instead of the wild intensity she expected from him, a gentle kiss followed his gentle, almost hesitant touches. He explored her mouth with soft sweeps of his tongue before pulling away to tenderly pressing his lips against hers. While she appreciated his restraint, Eleanor needed more. She bit down on his bottom lip, a gentle nip before releasing him.

As far as kisses went, it ranked right up there with the kiss between Wesley and Buttercup in *The Princess Bride*, but Eleanor wanted more from him. No. She needed more. For the first time she had an inkling about what the pack meant when they talked about mates. It wasn't just a strong emotion or a private vow. The bond between mates drilled deep and dug into the very essence of who they were.

"El, I need to hear you say it."

"Don't stop. This is right." She didn't hesitate or think about the words she spoke. The rightness of everything settled on her like a heavy blanket, keeping her warm from the cold and safe from the bogeyman.

She nipped at his collarbone, unsure of what came over her, but she had a desire to leave her mark on him.

Jackson didn't need to hear more. He leaned over her and his lips landed on hers again before moving down her neck to her collarbone where he left bites matching the ones she gave him.

His towel slipped from his hips and Eleanor glanced down. Jackson was large. His hands and feet, both large, proportionally fit with his body, but he was even bigger than she imagined. She'd seen him naked before, but she did her best to not gawk. Now that no one was around to tease her in front of Foster for gaping at Jackson, she appreciated the sight.

Planting his fists on either side of her head, Jackson pushed his body up. The muscles in his arms and shoulders bunched and flexed while his stomach coiled and the lines defining his muscles became more pronounced. If that was even possible.

"El," Jackson growled out through clenched teeth.

She lifted her admiring gaze away from his body and looked into his eyes. His beautiful glowing eyes that jumped between silver and jade. "Your wolf?"

"He's close. Been close all night."

Eleanor traced her fingertip over the bite on his collarbone. The mark was more pronounced and deeper than she thought she had made. What came over her? What did it matter? It was right. Jackson was right. *This* was right. She wished she could say all of that and more, but words wouldn't do her feelings justice.

"I know." Jackson nuzzled his nose against her neck. "I've known since the night you showed up here, but I didn't realize it until days later. But I know, Eleanor. *I know.*"

The weight of his words settled on her chest like the heavy weight she had sometimes felt pressing against her chest when Jackson wanted

Foster to do something without spending a half hour playing the why game. Eleanor spent her adult life, although short, studying the idea of magic as it existed within folklore. She'd just assumed it didn't exist. Then Foster came into her life and her definition of magic shifted as she explained away his transformation from boy to wolf. Finally, Eleanor came to Broken Peak and her definition of magic changed yet again. What she felt right then, with Jackson, might not be magic in the traditional sense, or even the fairy tale sense found in movies and books, but it was no less real than gravity.

Jackson rolled to his side and rested his chin on his fist as he peered down at her. "You're thinking awfully hard about something."

"Good things," Eleanor smiled up at him as she wrapped her arms around his neck and pulled him back down for a kiss.

"Promise?"

"I swear."

"You'll tell me if your thoughts go somewhere else?"

"Cross my heart," she drew a cross over her heart with her fingers.

"You're overdressed. We need to fix that." He tugged at the bottom of her shirt and lifted it up over her head in a single motion. He didn't even have to fumble with lifting her up or getting her to raise her arms. One moment she had a shirt on and the next it was on the floor next to his towel.

Once bare to his gaze, Jackson stared down at her with an expression of wonder that bordered on reverence. He pressed his hand down over her heart, splaying his fingers over her breasts so the tip of his thumb and little finger rested on top of her nipples. "I won't hurt you, El. I would never hurt you. And I won't let my wolf claim you. At least not until you're ready. I swear."

"I know."

"You're beautiful," Jackson released a long breath, almost a sigh.

"You are a wonderful mother to my son. You are my mate. You are beautiful. And I am the luckiest wolf shifter in the world."

Eleanor blinked back the sting from the tears forming in the corners of her eyes. Jackson might not be the most poetic or romantic of men, but the conviction of his beliefs came complete with the subtle power she had learned came from the dominant nature of his wolf. Butterflies fluttered around her belly and dove lower and lower with each breath she took.

Jackson bent over her and kissed the skin around his hand. Her heart thudded against the palm of his hand and he closed his eyes. With his free hand he wove his fingers through hers and lifted her palm up against his chest just over his heart.

His heartbeat matched hers.

More magic.

Jackson slid down her body, kissing her exposed skin along the way but keeping his hand over her heart.

Eleanor didn't know where she wanted him or what she wanted him to do. All she understood was the flood of sensations building inside of her. The fluttering of butterfly wings. The tingling of anticipation. The steady beat of her heart. She arched her back, pressing her shoulders down on the bed and lifting her breasts towards Jackson if he hadn't moved down her body.

Jackson growled and laid his forearm over her waist and hips, keeping her from wiggling away from him. He looked up the length of her body and waited for Eleanor to look down at him. As soon as their gazes met, he smiled a wolfish grin, one that caused his eyes to glow more silver than green before lowering his head and spending an inordinate amount of attention on her belly button.

Enough was enough. Eleanor reached down, tangled her fingers through his hair and pulled him back up her body. He didn't need any urging and surged up the length of her body. Her legs parted to accommodate his size and her hips cradled his.

Jackson's lips found hers, covering her with kisses. "I promise I'll take care of you."

Eleanor pressed her hands against the smooth skin of his cheeks and pressed her mouth against his. She enjoyed the kisses too much to be distracted by words. Her lips parted and his tongue invaded while his hands covered her breasts. He worked his fingers over her flesh before focusing on her nipples, gently rolling and pinching them between his thumb and forefingers. The gentle, but firm touches sent waves of pleasure through her body.

She moaned, and he did his low rumbling growl in response.

Her heart quickened its beat and his heartbeat echoed hers.

Jackson's lips, teeth, and tongue followed the path of his fingers, moving lower. Except this time, he paused only to kiss the small spot above her belly button before moving lower. "These have got to go."

Hooking a finger through the side of her panties, he ripped through the seam and pulled them from her body. They too ended on the floor next to the towel and the shirt. His fingers and mouth found their goal at the same time. His tongue and teeth worked her clit while his fingers pushed into her.

"So wet, El. Is this for me?"

Eleanor groaned, or maybe she moaned, and banged her head back against the pillow. She was focusing too much on what Jackson was doing to her, the feelings and sensations he drew from her body to concentrate on answering his question. Even if the answer entailed a single word consisting of three letters. She lifted her hips up off the bed and pressed her feet down flat on the mattress, opening herself up to his attentions even more.

Jackson slipped a third finger inside of her, slowly moving his hand in time with the lapping of her tongue against her sensitive clit. She didn't think it was possible, but Jackson increased the pleasure building up inside her. Her thighs tightened in anticipation, and she lifted up even further off the bed. As though getting closer to his lips and fingers could push her over the edge of release even sooner.

Except her release wasn't part of Jackson's plans. Just before she catapulted over and shattered from the intensity of the pleasure he gave her, he pulled away. Jackson surged up her body again, but hooked his arm under her knee and brought her leg up as the head of his hard cock pushed against her, teasing her with what was about to come.

Jackson kissed her again, swallowing her moans of frustration as he reached between them and guided the length of his hard shaft into her an inch at a time. He was larger than anything Eleanor had experienced before and the way he stretched her body danced lightly along the pain threshold without ever crossing over. But she didn't care. She wanted everything he had to give her and more.

Sliding her hands across and down his back to his hips, she pressed her hands into his barely yielding flesh and dug her fingers into the hard muscles of his ass. With her hands firmly in place, Eleanor jerked her hips upward and pulled Jackson's hips down hard.

Jackson's muscles tensed up as his body froze and he ground his molars together, "woman..."

Eleanor enjoyed the feeling of Jackson filling her so completely to laugh at his eyes crossing while he slowly gained back control. She wasn't going to make it easy for him. Before he could list the third digit of a random but obscure point of data, Eleanor lowered her hips before thrusting them back up with even more force than before.

Jackson squeezed his eyes shut and didn't bother biting back the growl. Eleanor's hands kept him pressed against her so when she circled her hips, the base of his cock rubbed up against her clit.

"El, baby," Jackson groaned as he nuzzled her neck and nibbled her earlobe, "you feel so good. So tight. So right."

He gave up holding himself back and pulled out of her completely before slamming back into her with a hard thrust. Jackson didn't move any faster, but each thrust was strong and hard. His arm slipped around the back of her knee and he bent forward, giving him even deeper penetration.

Their hips rolled against one another as their pleasure climbed to new peaks together. As their bodies moved in tandem and they neared the precipice of surrendering to the pleasure building within them, Eleanor tightened around him. She wanted to wait for him, but Jackson's movements were too much for her.

Eleanor fell over the edge, her body shattering as she bit down on Jackson's shoulder to keep the scream of pleasure from waking everyone. Jackson exploded, his own release immediately following hers. Her body slick from perspiration, she struggled to catch her breath as the waves of pleasure continued to roll through her.

Jackson collapsed on top of, but kept his weight off his body before rolling off to the side. She followed his roll, facing him with a shy smile.

"We need to keep things as normal as possible for Foster."

Jackson shook his head and chuckled, "woman, I love that our son is your priority, but that's the first thing you're going to say to me after that? And after this?" He pointed to the bite she left behind on the top of his shoulder at the base of his neck. It wasn't just a love bite, Eleanor had broken his skin.

"Holy sugar!" She squinted her eyes and leaned in closer to better examine the mark. "I did that?"

"Yep," Jackson was too proud, "you bit me real good."

Eleanor leaned back and peered up into his eyes. The eyes that hadn't stopped glowing once. His wolf was close. Had been the entire time. But his wolf seemed just as proud. She closed one eye and pursed her lips together. She didn't expect him to be angry or upset, but she hadn't expected his chest to swell with pride. "Jackson…"

"Mate. It's halfway to being all official now."

"What?" Eleanor screeched and sat up in bed. "What do you mean exactly by the word halfway?"

"Well, Vixen didn't bite Bray and claim him back until much later, so maybe halfway isn't the right term." The words coming from Jackson made no sense. She understood the meaning of each word, but when Jackson strung them together, that understanding went out the window.

"Jackson…" She did her best impression of a growl back at him.

He just laughed, wrapped his arms around her, and pulled her down next to him. His body curled around hers, pressing his chest against her back and keeping her warm with his body heat. "Relax. I'm not sure it works the same way for humans. We'll do the conversating thing in the morning. I promise. But right now, I need you in bed with me where I know you're safe."

"Jackson? Why do you need to know I'm safe?" She tried to turn around in his arms to face him, but his strong embrace kept her in place while he nuzzled the nape of her neck. The entire time, his chest vibrated with a soft rumble of satisfaction.

"We'll explain everything in the morning, I swear." His teeth nipped at her skin, teasing her with the promise of harder bites in the future.

"Is Foster safe?" How had she forgotten about Foster?

"I checked on him before coming here. Finley shifted and is sleeping in bed with him. If I didn't trust he was safe, I would have brought him in here with us." Jackson wrapped his leg around her so her body was enveloped by his.

Satisfaction and contentment settled down on her. The sense that everything was at it should be pushed aside the questions brewing in her mind.

"Jackson?"

"Yeah?" He pressed a kiss to her shoulder and hugged her tight.

"This is right."

"I know," Jackson whispered in response.

CHAPTER NINETEEN

JACKSON added an orange slice to the plate he prepared Eleanor for breakfast. An orange slice he added a fucking twist to because he remembered seeing it on a plate in a restaurant once. Thank God the rest of the pack and Foster were sleeping off their sugar comas.

"Vi is doing her interrogation thing with our uninvited guests." Bray leaned against the kitchen doorway with his arms crossed over his chest.

"Let me drop this off for El then I'll come and help?"

"Nah, she wants to do this alone." Bray pushed off the wall and stepped into the kitchen, "have you told her yet?"

"Told who what yet?"

"Did you tell Eleanor about last night?

"Not the specifics, no…" Jackson pressed his hands down on top of the counter and tucked his chin to his chest. "Not planning on it either. She doesn't need to know."

"Yes, she does."

"What? That I'm a killer? That I killed a man?" Jackson spun to face his Alpha and fisted his hands at his side. Sometimes the prick of his claws against the flesh of his palms was enough to stop him from doing something stupid.

"No. That you did what you had to do to keep your pup and her safe. And that you'll do it again. Like Vi says, rip the band-aid off. If Eleanor can't handle the darker side of shifters, the violent part, whatever bond you have with her claiming mark will fray and break apart if it's based on lies." Bray bent his head toward Jackson's neck.

Even with the neat little trick of healing faster than normal, the mark was still there. If Jackson had any doubts about the claiming thing going both ways when a human was involved, they left the minute he woke up that morning and saw the mark in the mirror. "Not telling her isn't the same as telling a lie."

"No, it's worse."

"How is it worse?"

"I don't know, but it is. Or that's what Vi says, I haven't figured it all out. It makes sense when she says it though." Bray crossed the kitchen floor and poured himself a cup of coffee from the fresh pot Jackson had just brewed for Eleanor. "Look at it this way. If she doesn't get spooked, you two will be perfect and if she freaks out, well, you'll probably have until Foster's eighteen to convince her to not be spooked."

"That makes no sense." Jackson pinched the bridge of his nose between his thumb and forefinger. "You know, I liked you better when you didn't give us advice."

"Yeah, but would you rather be talking with me or with Vi?"

Jackson shook his head from side to side. "You're both equally bad, but for different reasons."

"Tell her. And tell her sooner rather than later. Vi hasn't shared her plans for our guests. With your luck, she'll invite them to dinner and then Church's name will come up and you'll have to explain what happened in front of an audience." Bray reached for a slice of apple deemed unfit for Eleanor's consumption and popped it into his mouth.

"And what am I going to tell her? Hey, El, guess what? I'm a killer. I am a cold-blooded murderer. I let my wolf out, knowing what will happen, and don't regret it at all? And what's she going to say to that? Huh?" Jackson gesticulated wildly, reinforcing his words by swinging his arms around.

"She's going to ask why you didn't tell her last night." Eleanor's soft voice floated into the kitchen.

Jackson closed his eyes and inhaled through his nose. Yep, he smelled her fresh and clean scent mingled with a hint of fear. "Is this what you were trying to warn me about?"

Bray shrugged and grabbed another apple slice before heading out of the kitchen. He paused for a moment to give Eleanor a quick nod, "we'll keep Foster distracted you two talk as long as you need."

"Well? Why didn't you tell me last night?" Eleanor asked.

Jackson took another deep breath and turned to face her. She stood in the doorway, wearing one of his t-shirts. It was so big on her, the bottom came down to the top of her knees and the collar hung loosely from her shoulders. He really liked the way she looked in his clothes. Maybe he could hide the clothes she brought with her. And then change Vixen's passwords so Eleanor couldn't order any new clothes. "You're afraid."

"Not of you."

"Don't lie, El. I can tell, remember?"

"I'm not afraid of you, Jackson." Eleanor stepped into the kitchen, reinforcing her words. "The last thing you'd do is hurt Foster and if you hurt me, it will devastate Foster. It's not the perfect reason to not fear someone, but it's unimpeachable." She took another few steps until she was inches away from him.

"So explain the fear."

"No. You haven't answered my question."

"I..." Jackson opened his mouth, prepared to deliver some excuse about protecting her, but the words wouldn't come out. His head dropped and his shoulders slumped. He opted for the truth instead of the excuse. "I was protecting myself. I was scared you'd leave me. Leave the pack if you knew."

"Knew what?" She slipped closer to him and lifted her chin to better see his eyes. "That you killed someone? Considering what Vixen shared and why you and Bray were on patrol and your condition when you came back, don't you think I'd at least ask what he was doing here?"

The words spilled out in quick succession with no pause for breath between them. "My wolf killed him, but I could have stopped it if I wanted. I didn't stop it, so I must have wanted it too."

"Jackson," Eleanor reached for his hands and held them both between hers. He couldn't believe she was touching him after she heard his inadvertent confession. "What was he doing here?"

He closed his eyes and shook his head from side to side, "promise me you won't take Foster and run, El, please. Just promise me you won't do that, I can't survive that."

"Have a little faith in me, Jackson." She lifted his hands to her mouth and pressed her lips against his knuckles.

"We overheard them, Bray and me, they were going to take Foster."

She dropped his hands, and he expected her to run, but she didn't. Eleanor paced the width of the kitchen, muttering something under her breath about just wanting to see them try. His mate was brave and fierce for a human.

Jackson didn't bother hiding his grin and his wolf didn't bother to hide his pride. He watched her walk from wall to wall, avoiding the furniture while she listed off the different ways she would destroy anyone who even tried to touch her son.

God, his mate was gorgeous when she got all protective of their son.

His mate.

Their son.

Jackson rolled the words around in his mind. They sounded nice.

Right. Like she had said to him last night. It was just right.

He was a fool for doubting her. Eleanor raised a little wolf all on her own for almost four years. Of course she was strong and resilient and brave and all the things he wasn't when it came to her. Maybe she'd give him lessons if he asked nicely. Jackson bet she was an excellent teacher too. His mind immediately played images of Eleanor dressed up as a teacher with glasses and a tight skirt and her hair up in a bun. Except, Eleanor didn't have long hair. She wore her hair about chin length. Oh, pulled back in a headband. Even better.

"Jackson?" Eleanor had stopped her pacing at some point during his fantasizing and from the exasperation in her voice and twitching eyebrow, she'd said his name a few times before he heard her.

"Yeah?" He wore a goofy grin, the same one Vixen liked to tease him about when she caught him staring at Eleanor when he thought she wasn't looking. It was inappropriate, but he didn't much care at the moment.

"You said they."

"Yeah?"

"But you also said you only killed one." She narrowed her eyes, planted her hands on her hips, and tapped her toe against the floor.

Jackson was right. Even in a t-shirt, the woman pulled off the school teacher attitude. He moved around the kitchen, using the excuse of finishing making her breakfast to hide his erection, made more obvious by the loose pair of pajama pants he pulled on when he got out of bed earlier. The time was inappropriate to get hard, but try telling his dick that. "Bray and I caught three men. I killed one, but Bray caught the other two. We brought them back and secured them in the shed before I found you last night. There was no way they could have escaped."

He needed to work on his bravery. Sure, he turned his back to her to hide his erection, but he also kept his back to her because he'd seen the look of disappointment she used with Foster. The tight and pursed lips with narrowed eyes destroyed Jackson when it wasn't aimed at him. He didn't want to consider the obstacle course his emotions would have to tackle if she leveled that expression on him.

Drawers slammed open and closed. The sound of the contents banging against each other echoed through the room, distracting Jackson from putting the finishing touches on the fruit plate. He turned his head to the side, watching Eleanor stare at the innards of a drawer before slamming it closed and opening the next one. "Whatcha doing?"

"Where are the knives? Not these little paring knives. I want a big knife. One with a really long blade. Like the ones you and the others wear sometimes. Like the one you had last night."

Jackson saw the wheels turn in Eleanor's brain and the imaginary light bulb light up above her head. She turned on her heel and speed walked down the hallway to Jackson's bedroom.

Their bedroom. He corrected himself, even if no one else heard his thoughts.

She was halfway down the hallway before he caught up with her. The sway of her hips from side to side had distracted him enough to slow down his progress. He wrapped his hand around her elbow and pulled her back against him. "Whoa there, El. Where do you think you're going?"

"I'm going to teach those men in the shed a lesson. No one, and I mean no one, threatens my son."

She wriggled out of his grasp, but he caught her around her waist and pulled her back before she made it to their room and found a knife. Or another weapon. As much as his wolf enjoyed the image of his mate going after the uninvited guests, Vixen wouldn't appreciate the interruption to her interrogation.

"El, baby, slow down." He lifted her up off the ground and her feet dangled in the air with her heels batting away at his shins. "Vixen is getting answers from them right now. Once she learns what she needs, she'll share it with us. If you still want time with them, we'll make sure you have it."

Her feet stopped swinging, and she hung limply over his forearm. "Promise?"

"I promise, El." He rubbed his cheek against the side of her head and closed his eyes taking in her scent.

"Are you sniffing my hair?"

"Yep, and there are plenty of other things I plan on sniffing too." Jackson didn't see the point in hiding it from her. He pivoted, keeping Eleanor against his chest, and retraced their steps back to the kitchen. "But before we get to that, I need to feed you. Then we're going back to our room since Bray promised to entertain Foster and take advantage of some uninterrupted grown-up time."

"Are you trying to distract me?"

"Yep." Jackson dropped Eleanor on the counter and handed her the fruit plate. "Is it working?"

"I don't know," she picked up a strawberry and bit into it, "I'll tell you when I finish breakfast."

Jackson stared at Eleanor's mouth. His wolf took inspiration from Eleanor's words and was clawing his way out, wanting to get to the two men held in the shed. As much as he wanted to distract Eleanor from running off, he also needed to distract his wolf from taking over.

ELEANOR UNDERSTOOD THE LOGIC BEHIND VIXEN'S DECISION, BUT SHE didn't agree with it. Both Bray and Vixen had sat down with Eleanor and explained the many reasons for letting the two men leave the territory, but she didn't like any of them. What she hated most about the entire situation was that Vixen was preparing for an attack. But if the men did as promised, and delivered the message to leave Vixen and all the other shifters alone, not just the pack at Broken Peak, why did they need to watch the borders?

And worse, they overruled Eleanor's desire to keep Foster indoors. No one admitted it, but she figured they hoped to use her son to tempt whoever ordered Foster's abduction into acting. Sure, it made sense, but only when it wasn't her son who was part of the plan. But then Vixen had done her whole do you trust me speech and all of Eleanor's doubts faded away. Well, they faded away whenever she was around Vixen. As soon as Vixen ran off to check out something one of the pack found on their patrols, the doubts returned.

"It's okay to be nervous, but Foster will sense it. Why don't you spend some time looking through Mac's great grandma's journals?" Roose grumbled out in his baritone voice from his spot next to her on the porch swing.

They'd been swinging back and forth in silence for the past thirty minutes. Roose showed up at the Lodge and the first clue he wasn't stopping by for a neighborly visit was claiming he wanted to talk with

Eleanor. The second clue was the rest of the pack heading out with horrible excuses like having to check the overgrowth on some game trails. The only thing that settled Eleanor's already frayed nerves was Foster playing in the yard. Since he wasn't technically in school, the least she could do for an education that included homeschooling, was give him a small head start. Currently, that head start included collecting different leaves they would identify when the tree encyclopedia Vixen ordered arrived.

"Mommy look!" Foster waved his hands in the air above his head. At first glance she thought he found a stick, which definitely wasn't a leaf, but this stick moved. A lot.

"I'll take care of it," Roose chuckled in his low rumbling way that caused everything around him to shake and pushed off the swing. "Foster, did you check the snake's colors? Remember what Mac taught you?"

"It's a milkshake!"

"It's a milk snake, Foster, a milk *snake*." Eleanor closed her eyes and counted to three. A milk snake might not be venomous, but Eleanor wouldn't be surprised if it bit Foster. No one enjoyed swinging in the air the way that poor snake was. And from the look the snake gave Roose as he approached conveyed its desire to be released from the four-year-old tyrant. By the time Roose freed the snake, that was as long as Foster was tall, another leaf blew across the yard in need of collecting and Foster forgot all about the snake.

At least it wasn't a copperhead again. Foster found one sunbathing on some rocks a few days ago and despite the hyper-vigilant adults surrounding the boy, he still picked it up. One minute Jackson was talking with her and the next he was racing across the yard, saving Foster from a bite. They reassured her that shifters fought off copperhead venom like most humans fought off colds. It made no difference to Eleanor's nerves, and she recruited Mac to give Foster lessons on identifying and leaving alone the timber rattlesnakes and copperheads. On the bright side, they were too far north to contend with water moccasins. She hoped.

After releasing the poor snake close to the woods, Roose made his way back to the porch and her. "I need to head out soon. You going to be okay?"

Eleanor nodded, "as well as can be. Besides, someone will find an excuse to swing by and check that I haven't panicked and locked us in the bathroom. Again." In a moment of complete irrationality at hearing a shriek that turned out to be Vixen's griffin, which Eleanor and Foster still hadn't seen yet, Eleanor scooped up Foster and ran to safety. It took Jackson, along with Bray and Vixen, to convince her to unlock the door.

"No one blames you for that, little mother. That scream is enough to make anyone run and hide." Roose rubbed his shoulder against a post on the porch. Jackson explained Roose didn't realize he was marking the lodge, and normally Bray would have challenged Roose. But ever since the threat to Foster, everyone in the Broken Peak region, even the few shifters Eleanor hadn't met, gave their animals more control. "You know the drill if anything happens?"

Eleanor lifted the radio and waved it in the air. "It's already set to channel 11. I just have to push the button and say the word silver and everyone comes running."

The radio crackled just as she finished reciting the directions for what to do if she noticed anyone or anything uninvited. Eleanor wondered if the milk snake counted as uninvited while lifting the radio to her ear.

"Hey, El, how about Finley and I swing by and grab, Foster for some wolf time?"

Either Foster heard the crackle of the radio or Jackson's words, because he dropped the leaves and charged to the porch, pumping his legs with his knees high, as though that would make him run faster. But what did Eleanor know, maybe it did.

"Can I? Can I? Huh? Can I, pleassssse?"

Eleanor understood few absolute truths in her life. One was that Foster would be safe with Jackson, no matter what. The only reason they left Foster at home during their patrols was because the males couldn't focus on their task if they had a four-year-old constantly asking questions. She didn't need to think about her answer. "Sure, want to tell him?"

Foster jumped up and down in front of her and she took it to mean an enthusiastic yes. She held the radio up to Foster's mouth and pressed the talk button. After the first attempt with the radio took over thirty minutes because Foster had difficulty pressing the talk button and speaking at the same time, Eleanor took over the technical details of father and son communicating through a military grade radio.

"Daddy, daddy, daddy, guess what?"

"-hat?" Eleanor lifted her finger from the talk button a second too slow and the first letter of Jackson's response was cut off. Not that it made a difference to her son, though she never knew when Foster was done speaking or if he had a few more sentences to add.

"Mommy said yes? Can you believe it? Can you? Can you? Can you?" Eleanor released the talk button on the second can you, saving Jackson and everyone else's ears.

"Okay. Finley and I will swing by and pick you up. Be ready to go in a few minutes."

The radio went silent and Foster raced back into the yard where he ran around in fast circles. There wasn't a lot of preparation needed for wolf time, so she let him run around to his heart's content until Jackson arrived.

True to his promise, Jackson and Finley arrived a few minutes later and Roose waved goodbye to everyone as he trotted in the opposite direction of their arrival. Jackson strode across the yard, patting Foster on the head as Jackson passed him on his way to Eleanor. As soon as he reached her, Jackson wrapped his arms around her waist and lifted her up against his body.

"I've missed you, El."

"It's only been a few hours," she giggled at his admission, feeling very much like a teenager and not a grown-up woman with a four-year-old son.

"Yeah, but I still missed you."

"That's good, because in the immortal words of David Cassidy, I think I love you." As soon as the words came out of her mouth, Eleanor wished she could stick them back in. It was one thing to tell Jackson that it felt right when she was with him, but it was something else to use the L Word.

Jackson's eyes glowed that silvery greenish color as he stared at her with a hunger in his eyes that Eleanor had come to appreciate for what it led to. Although it hadn't happened as often as she would have liked because of patrols and a certain four-year-old who found any number of reasons to fall asleep in Jackson's bed, well, more or less their bed now.

"Say that again?"

"What? That it's good?"

Jackson nipped at her bottom lip, "woman, don't tempt me after I made a promise to our son."

That was one of the many reasons Eleanor loved Jackson; he always put Foster ahead of everyone and thing. "Very well, Jackson, I think I love you."

"Good. Because I love you too, Eleanor Ward, I figured we'd have to wait until Foster hit puberty before you'd admit it."

"You didn't want to say it first?"

"Daddy!" Foster did his running in circle thing in front of the porch steps while squealing in that high-pitched voice of his and punching and kicking at the air. "It's wolf time!"

"Go," Eleanor slid down Jackson's body and planted a soft kiss on the mark at his neck, "before your son loses his mind."

"Why don't you take the quiet time to read some of those journals." Jackson planted another kiss on her forehead, before scooping Foster up under an arm and walking into the woods with a quick glance over his shoulder and a wave goodbye.

Eleanor took Jackson's advice and ventured inside to get the journals Mac kept on dropping off when he found another in storage and the laptop Vixen ordered to keep her research in order. As soon as she returned to the porch and settled on the swing, she dove into the journals. All was quiet for about five minutes and then the noises happened. Nothing out of the ordinary for the woods, but the cracking branches and rustling leaves raised the hairs on her arms.

Something, or someone, was out there. But then, Eleanor was convinced an uninvited guest, as Vixen called them, caused every odd noise. Usually, Foster was around when she noticed the sounds, so she ignored them. But now she was alone and keeping Foster safe didn't mean keeping close to the house with him. She set her work down on the swing and with a deep breath stood and looked in the direction the sounds came from.

Probably nothing, or worse than nothing, a rabbit or squirrel racing through the woods. But until she checked it out, she'd be paranoid and wouldn't get any work done. Without a second thought, Eleanor jogged down the porch steps and across the yard to the woods. She stopped close to fifteen feet away from the edge where the woods became a forest and stared into the trees. As though she could even see anything.

It wasn't like her human eyes gave her the same acuity of sight as Jackson or the others.

Nothing.

Of course it was nothing. Her mind was playing tricks on her. She turned and headed back to the porch, swearing she wouldn't let normal forest noises distract her again. At the halfway point, a loud snap, like a branch breaking off from a tree, came from behind her, but she didn't stop to look.

Her calf burned with a pain she'd never experienced before and her legs went out from underneath her.

What the-

Black combat boots crossed her field of vision before everything turned dark. Whoever was there put a hood over her head, blocking her sight. But she didn't need to see to know who it was. She might not know their name or serial number or rank, but she knew whoever had shot her, at least she assumed that's what happened since the pain hadn't gone away and her legs felt wet, was an uninvited guest. She assumed he was part of a team sent to grab her son.

"Eleanor Ward, we don't want to hurt you any more than we had to. Cooperate and this will all be over before you realize it."

CHAPTER TWENTY

AT THE sound of the gunshot, Finley and Jackson lifted their snouts to the sky and sniffed the air.

Blood. Human blood. Eleanor's blood. Jackson knew her scent as well as, if not better, than the individuals in his pack.

Jackson released a sharp bark, calling Foster away from the riverbed where he had been playing with a turtle. He didn't need to. The pup had already given up on the turtle and was crawling with his belly low to the ground toward Finley and Jackson. Foster whined and curled around Jackson's legs, seeking the comfort of his father. Jackson bent forward and licked the top of Foster's head.

Jackson wanted to chase down the source of the gunshot, but he wouldn't leave the pup alone and he couldn't bring the pup with him. Finley growled low and paced around Jackson and Foster. Just as Jackson wouldn't leave the pup, Finley wouldn't leave Jackson to fight off any threats alone.

Finley stopped his pacing and stared at Jackson, waiting for the older wolf to give him some kind of direction.

Jackson wasn't any help. The wolf's mind was a jumbled mess of thoughts. Torn between keeping his pup safe and needing to check on his mate, Jackson wasn't much help in keeping his beast in check. He needed to know someone was out there looking for Eleanor and then he could focus on Foster. He needed someone else to make the decisions.

Vixen. Where was Vixen? She had promised that no harm would come to Foster, but she forgot about Eleanor. Both Jackson and Eleanor needed Vixen. Griffin or female, it didn't matter which.

A sharp cry from above called to the wolves. As their eyes looked for the source, a large shadow blocked the light of the sun followed by a gust of wind that blew the leaves and loose dirt in a tight circle around the wolves. Foster whined softly and scooted back further under Jackson. The griffin hadn't met Foster yet, and this wasn't the best time for an introduction.

As the griffin came to a hard and clumsy landing, her takeoff skills being much better, a massive black wolf charged into the clearing and sat in front of the other wolves, facing the griffin. At least Bray was there. While Bray wasn't the griffin's Alpha, she paid attention to him. Soon after, the others arrived. Leighton and Allard came first, then Tevin and Roose with Mac riding Roose's bear.

"The cats are joining us. Gareth is calling those who are close by and I sent out the call to all the shifters outside Broken Peak." Mac slipped off Roose's back and looked around at the others before settling his gaze on Jackson. He tucked his hands into his deep pockets and narrowed his eyes in concentration. "We'll do what's necessary to keep them from leaving the Peak, but if one of them steps one foot outside of this territory, they won't make it a mile before they are caught."

Bray lifted his head and released a long howl of agreement.

Roose stood up on his hind legs and bellowed out a roar.

Vixen stroked her wings, hovering a few feet above the ground as she released a scream that penetrated the thick woods of the forest.

Anyone within hearing distance, human or shifter, would understand the message.

The shifters of Broken Peak were heading to battle.

And the shifters of the world? They were going to war.

CHAPTER TWENTY-ONE

VIXEN struggling to pull her griffin back and tuck her away beneath her human skin was painful to watch, but not anywhere close to the pain of watching her stalk and kill each human she encountered on the trek back to the house. Five total and not one went quickly. Quietly? Yes. Vixen silenced them all so at least the pack, following in her wake, didn't have to hear their screams of terror and pain.

They imagined them instead.

Eventually, the scent of blood was too much for the wolves and the pack all shifted back except for Bray. In order to keep their advantage, one of them had to stay in wolf form and Bray fell on the sword for the others. At least they didn't have to worry about the pup panicking at the scent of blood. Roose had taken Foster to Gareth. The mountain lion shifter was solitary but brutal and would protect the boy at all costs. Especially since Gareth was Wayne and Victor's cousin.

After the last body dropped to the ground in a bloody heap, Bray pushed Vixen toward the shed. The shed that would soon be burned to the ground because no way in hell was Jackson willing to allow any building to remain standing if it was involved in causing Eleanor harm. It made better sense when it was a figment and hadn't become a fully formed idea. Regardless, the shed would be burned down and hopefully filled with all the bodies Vixen was leaving behind.

"Why are you all just standing here?" Roose whispered from behind them.

Mac and the entire pack, except for Bray and Vixen who had scouted ahead, jumped at the sound.

"Vixen told us to wait," Finley whispered back.

"And you just started listening to her tonight?"

Finley pointed at the disemboweled body and kicked the limp arm with his toe. "*This* wasn't caused by her griffin. I think it's safe to say if she asks us to dress up in the Halloween costumes again and recreate the choreography from Macho Man, we will and we'll do it with a fucking smile."

Roose lifted a shoulder and sort of nodded in understanding.

Jackson leaned back on his heels. Staying still while knowing Eleanor was being held somewhere, hurt and frightened, killed his patience with a rusty screwdriver. He needed to go after her. He needed to find her. Roose dropped his hand down on Jackson's shoulder and his knees practically buckled under the weight. For everyone else, it looked like a gesture of support. Only Roose and Jackson understood it for what the hand on Jackson's shoulder was: a physical restraint keeping him from running.

"I can't..."

Roose's fingers tightened down on Jackson's shoulder and he lowered his mouth to Jackson's ear, whispering at a volume only Jackson heard. "You can and you will. Vixen is her best chance."

Before Roose had to dig his fingers in any deeper, Bray's massive black wolf slipped through the tree trunks and sat in front of the humans. The wolf cocked his head to the side and stared at Jackson. It would be so much easier to communicate if Bray's wolf conveyed his thoughts to the others. Instead, they relied on body language.

Bray's hackles weren't raised, and he wasn't snarling. Good signs. Or so Jackson hoped as he lifted his chin and pulled away from Roose. The wolf stood and turned in the direction he came from. When the others didn't immediately follow, he looked over his shoulder and grumbled out a soft growl. He also rolled his eyes, but that gesture was easier to identify when the human counterpart was doing it.

Jackson didn't care if the others were behind him or not. He strode forward and raised his arm and rested it on Bray's back, urging the wolf forward. The time for waiting was over and Jackson wanted his mate back. Jackson half-expected Bray to lead them to one of the many caves within the territory, or a tent erected in the middle of the woods, instead they approached the shed from the west. The same shed where Jackson and Bray left the two uninvited guests for Vixen to interview. Whoever ordered the men back into Broken Peak territory had a sick sense of humor.

Vixen waited, leaning against a tree. The casual pose belied the tension of her muscles, ready to spring at the slightest provocation. Bray stopped a few feet away, but Jackson continued until he stood next to Vixen.

"Why are you out here and not in there?" Jackson hissed.

Vixen lifted her knife and pointed at the door, "listen."

Jackson stared at the shed and narrowed his eyes. Listen? Listen for what? The sound of some asshole hurting El? His mind imagined the worst, Eleanor bruised and bloody. And then his ears picked up what Vixen wanted him to hear. Eleanor was yelling at whoever was inside with her. No other sounds accompanied the insults she hurled with great creativity and imagination. Her insults made Don Rickles seem like Mr. Rogers.

"They come out every twenty minutes or so. Like shooting fish in a barrel." Vixen swung her arm in an arc, pointing out all the incapacitated bodies with the tip of her knife.

Jackson kept his gaze locked on the door, waiting for the next man to emerge. "You killed them all?"

"Yes. Well, all but one."

"Why?"

Vixen breathed in deep through her nose then let the air out with a slow exhale, "I have my reasons. By my count there are two still in there. I am guessing they know something is wrong since no one who's left has returned."

"Do you have a plan, then?"

Vixen nodded, "just waiting for the signal."

"What signal?"

The radio on her belt released a low tone meant for only those close to the source. "That one. Gareth and Foster are secure. If this all goes pear shaped, which is a strong possibility, he's ready to take Foster and run to safety. Your kid might be raised by mountain lions, but at least he'll be safe."

Jackson turned his narrow-eyed gaze to Vixen, "my son will be raised by his mother and me."

"We're going to have a conversation about planning for eventualities, but that can wait. Right now, I'm going to teach you the proper way to kick the asses of those who dare to threaten what is yours." She stared ahead at the closed door and for the first time, Jackson understood Vixen's claim that she wasn't a good woman. The griffin wasn't the instrument of death the pack believed her to be. Vixen was the instrument of death.

Spinning the knife in the palm of her hand, Vixen pushed off the tree and strode across the clearing to the front of the shed, whistling the theme song to *The Good, the Bad, and the Ugly*. Bray's wolf came forward and stopped next to Jackson, butting his hand with the wolf's snout.

Jackson glanced over at the wolf, "she's your mate, man. You chose her."

The wolf opened his jaws and let his tongue hang out, as though saying, *yeah she is*.

Jackson and Bray hurried after Vixen. They didn't know her plan, but they wouldn't leave her alone, no matter how bat shit crazy she was. Turned out, she didn't need any backup.

"What's happening! Friggin' sugar jets, someone tell me what's happening!" Eleanor, bound to a chair with her arms behind her and her ankles tied to the chair legs and a black hood over her head, yelled from her corner of the shed.

Jackson took a quick inventory of Eleanor's state. She might be angry, but he could still smell blood, her blood. She didn't appear to be physically harmed, but Jackson could put two and two together, even in his panicked state. The sound of the gunshot plus the scent of Eleanor's blood meant she had a bullet wound somewhere on her body.

Meanwhile, Vixen kicked, threw punches, butted heads, and stomped feet. Despite the knife in her hand, she didn't use the pointy end against the remaining two assailants. The blood she drew from the men was earned with her fists.

The thumping of Eleanor's chair distracted Jackson from watching the fight. He always knew Vixen was capable. When she first arrived, wounded and scared, she put Jackson to his knees by twisting his arm and hitting the right nerve in his wrist. She could hold her own. Besides, Bray hadn't shifted back. The Alpha wolf would be a formidable ally if

Vixen got into trouble, which Jackson figured would be unlikely given the state of the two men inside the shed.

Jackson rushed across the small area to the corner and knelt in front of Eleanor. He ran his hands over her shoulders, down her arms, inspected each of her fingers, then dragged his hands along her legs to her ankles. As his hand slid along her calf, Eleanor stopped her string of pseudo curses long enough to wince.

He found the bullet wound.

"It's okay El, I'm going to get you out of here."

"What? Jackson? Is that you?" Eleanor swung her head from side to side. And even though he crouched right in front of her, she struggled to locate him with her head and face covered with a dark hood.

"Are you okay, El?" Jackson pulled the hood off with one hand, but kept his attention focused on her calf. He yanked up her jeans and Eleanor flinched again. "Tell me you're okay."

Eleanor looked down, her bottom lip trembled and her eyes grew big as they filled with tears, but she nodded.

Pain lanced at his stomach. Probably guilt. Jackson couldn't stand the look on her face and focused on the wound on her leg. "Gauze. Good. Does it hurt? Of course it hurts. I'm going to get you out of here, El. You're safe now and I swear, no one will ever hurt you again, I promise."

While he worked on the ropes tying her ankles to the chair, Jackson briefly wondered if Amazon had an outfit made of bubble wrap he could get for Eleanor. And Foster. When the knots proved too much for Jackson's lack of composure, his claws came out and he sliced through the rough hemp. However, when he circled around to her back, instead of finding her hands tied in place with rope, he discovered handcuffs. As powerful as his claws were against things like wood and heavy ropes, metal posed a problem.

Eleanor tugged at her arms, "hurry up. Vixen isn't going to leave anyone left for me. She's spinning, Jackson. Spinning. And her arms, holy criminy, she has to teach me how to do that!"

Jackson peeked over Eleanor's shoulder, and sure enough, Vixen appeared to be spinning. It was more following the two men attempting to evade her hands, feet, and Bray's teeth as he herded them back into Vixen's reach. Jackson glanced around the room, looking for keys to the handcuffs. They had to be somewhere. He hoped one of the men hadn't put the keys in a pocket, because he had no desire to run back outside and rifle through a bunch of dead men's pockets.

A shadow fell upon the shed, and Jackson looked toward the door. Roose ducked his head and walked into the one room building, carefully avoiding the fight in case he offended Vixen by inadvertently helping her. "What's taking so long?"

"Handcuffs." Both Jackson and Eleanor spoke at the same time. Both were impatient, but Jackson had a feeling Eleanor's impatience stemmed from her missing out on the chance to hit someone.

They'd be having a conversation about that later.

Roose lumbered across the floor and knelt behind the chair next to Jackson. "No keys?"

"If I had keys, do you think we'd still be here?"

"No, we'd be beating the sugar out of those idiots. Threaten me with taking away my son because it's what's best for him..." Eleanor leaned from side to side, taking the chair with her.

Roose and Jackson shared a look. Maybe it was better to keep the handcuffs on. Eleanor looked over her shoulder and down at Jackson.

"Well?"

Jackson held up both of his hands in mock surrender, "no keys."

"You have sharp pointy claws, pick them. If people can break out of handcuffs with a bobby pin, I don't see how they'd be too difficult for a pointy claw."

Roose shrugged his shoulders and lifted his arms in defeat. Apparently, even threatening to separate Eleanor from Foster was deserving of capital punishment. Not that Jackson didn't feel the same, but the claws, fangs, and nifty little trick of healing faster than humans gave him a stark advantage.

"Oh fer cryin' out loud, Vixen, stop toying with them and either kill 'em or knock 'em out or whatever." Mac's gruff voice came from the doorway.

Before anyone could protest, namely Eleanor, Vixen did as Mac suggested. Two quick strikes with the sharp end of her knife, and both men were dead. Not painful enough for Jackson's satisfaction, but at least they didn't need an excuse to keep Eleanor restrained. As soon as the bodies hit the ground, Roose grabbed hold of the chain between the cuffs and yanked the links apart.

Eleanor's arms fell to her sides, "ow."

"Yeah, give it a few minutes," Jackson stood behind Eleanor and rubbed her shoulders.

"Where's Foster?" Eleanor jumped to her feet, forgetting the wound in her calf. If Jackson hadn't grabbed her around the waist, she would have gone over. "If you're here, and so is everyone else, where's Foster."

"Gareth has him." Jackson hesitated, not sure what he should or could say about the mountain lion shifter. If he was Alpha, he could decide what to share, but he wasn't. Bray was. It was up to Bray and Vixen to decide.

"Who's that?" Eleanor hobbled around and looked up at Jackson. The bravery he'd seen earlier had been replaced with fear and panic. "Who is Gareth and why does he have Foster."

Mac looked over at Bray and Vixen, but neither of them were any condition to play the comforting role. Bray protectively circled Vixen while she stood in the center of the small room while she regained control. If the griffin made an appearance in the small shed, it would be a catastrophe. Leaving the two Alphas to their recovery, Mac shuffled across the floor to Eleanor while Roose dragged the dead bodies out of the shed.

"Gareth is Victor and Wayne's cousin. Distant cousin, a few times removed probably, but still family. They knew to contact me because of him. Right now he has Foster in a secure location and once Vixen calms down enough, she'll let him know that it's safe to bring him home."

Eleanor looked over at Vixen. She took in the heavy breathing, the closed eyes, the bowed head. And the blood. Even being a human, she had to notice the heavy iron scent hanging in the air. Jackson's arms tightened around her waist. Vixen had taught them all about adrenaline and using it to keep going when everything said to give up. She also warned them that as soon as the adrenaline faded, shock would hit. Sure enough, Eleanor collapsed against him and her body trembled. And not in the good way, like it did when he had her in bed with him.

He scooped her up and cradled her in his arms. "Come on, let's get you home. We need to look at your leg and get some food and drink in you. And once Foster comes back, you'll be ready to see him."

"I'm ready now."

"Trust me on this, El. He'll ask questions you don't want to answer." Jackson headed out the door of the shed and to the woods where the rest of the pack waited.

The others surrounded Eleanor and Jackson as they walked through the woods along the game trail to the lodge. Every few feet, one of them reached out and brushed a hand over Eleanor, as though needing the touch to confirm what their eyes saw. That Eleanor was alive and relatively well, all things considered. Jackson's wolf wasn't thrilled with the touching, but both man and wolf understood it. Eleanor was part of the pack as much as Jackson or any of the others. The attack on Eleanor was an attack on the pack.

By the time they reached the front door, Eleanor was close to nodding off. With the adrenaline gone, sheer will was the only thing keeping her conscious.

CHAPTER TWENTY-TWO

ELEANOR sat down next to Mac on the porch swing and handed him a cup of coffee. He had promised her more journals and more mysteries when she was feeling better. Since she could get out of bed and walk around without wincing, Eleanor decided she was feeling better. Plus, she needed something to focus her mind on or she would go crazy.

They had all given her the space she needed after being shot and kidnapped, but she couldn't spend the rest of her life worrying about what might have happened. She never told Jackson, but she trusted he would find her and save her. And she believed with every part of her being that he would bring hell with him when he arrived. She just didn't realize hell would be a one woman killing machine.

As soon as Vixen got back to the house, but before she let Gareth know he could bring Foster back, she kicked everyone out of Eleanor's room and delivered a quick lecture. She pointed out the symptoms of PTSD Eleanor needed to look out for and also pointed out that it was normal to refuse all outreaches of help. It would take time, more than days or weeks, before Eleanor found her way back to where she was before someone used her as a bargaining chip to get to her son. Before Vixen left Eleanor alone so Jackson could come back in the room to hover, the Alpha female delivered a slight reprimand. Vixen somehow understood Eleanor was upset with Vixen. And even though Eleanor knew it was irrational, and that given the situation she wouldn't have been able to cause harm to either of the two men, she would have liked the opportunity to walk away. Or not. Vixen robbed her of that choice. Vixen's chastisement made it difficult for Eleanor to hold on to her resentment.

The only thing I took from you today was a lifetime of guilt. Eleanor would keep those words with her forever.

The pack kept Foster distracted for the few days it took for her leg to heal enough to stop the curious questions of a four-year-old. And Mac relied on Edna's remedies to speed up the healing.

"Before Vixen, and you, I'd worry about a pup as young as Foster living with the pack. Tevin was the youngest one I brought, and he could at least feed himself if worse came to worst." Mac sipped his coffee and closed his eyes with a happy sigh. "But there aren't a better bunch of males to grow up around."

"You don't have to convince me to stay, Mac. Did Vixen put you up to this? She's been acting strange around me since..."

"Nope, not trying to convince you of anything. I was just making an observation. And Vixen is acting strange because, well as she says, she's not a good woman and you had a front-row seat to that. The weirdness will fade over time." Mac looked out across the yard and grinned at whatever he saw at the tree line.

"What do you see?"

"Nothin'. Just wondering what else might come out of those woods. Vixen added to the pack's physical strength and you add to its mental strength. Vixen's griffin moved all the stuff we cataloged as lore into the realm of fact." Mac reached under the swing, pulled out a box filled with leather-bound books, and set it between them. "These are the legends. The weird writings that previous generations claimed were prophecy."

Eleanor ran her fingers over the soft covers. There had to be at least twenty books in the box. Even if the content amounted to nothing more than gibberish, the books could still tell her about the people who wrote them. The books were nirvana. "Do any of them mention a griffin?"

"A few. I stuck a piece of paper in those." Mac patted her hand and stood. "I'll leave you to them. Plus, the boys should be back soon."

Mac stepped off the porch and headed to the woods with his coffee in hand, but Eleanor was too distracted by the books to care. The first one she opened had a piece of yellow paper stuck inside the cover. She carefully flipped through the pages looking for any references to griffins.

Eleanor didn't know how much time had passed, but she'd looked through three books by the time Jackson and Foster came out of the woods. They dressed alike, worn jeans and a t-shirt, but Eleanor didn't think they realized they were doing it.

"Mommy, Daddy and I found a trail and followed it. It went down to the river and across then back over to uncle Roose's."

Eleanor set the book down, marking her place, and reached for her now cool cup of coffee. Foster enjoyed sharing their exploits during their wolf time, and Eleanor enjoyed listening to him.

As Foster babbled on about the different scents and sights. Jackson grinned at Eleanor and gave her a wink before patting Foster on the top of his head. "Okay, go and get washed up and ready for dinner. I think it's chili night."

"Okay!" Foster ran to the door and pulled it open, but didn't go inside the house right away. Instead, he turned to Jackson. Foster's forehead wrinkled in the telltale sign he was thinking hard about something. After a few seconds he closed an eye and tilted his head to the side, as though examining Jackson. "Can I call you Daddy? I don't use Mommy's name, and I don't want you to get jealous."

Eleanor looked away and wiped a finger under her eye. Out of the mouth of babes. She and Jackson had shared a few conversations about how to handle the whole dad and mom and relationship thing and Foster took care of one of their concerns.

Jackson nodded, taking a moment to get his emotions in check before opening his mouth. "I think I'd like that, son."

"Good. Oh. And since you're Mommy's, when are you going to make her yours."

Eleanor choked back a laugh and Jackson covered his laugh with a cough.

"What do you mean by that?" Jackson leaned against the porch railing and dug his hands into his pockets.

"Mommy marked you." Foster pointed at the bite mark visible on Jackson's neck. "You need to mark her. And that way you won't just be Mommy and Daddy, but my mommy and daddy."

"You'd be okay with that?"

Foster bobbed his head up and down, "yep."

Well, okay then. Apparently Jackson and Eleanor didn't need to worry. Foster had it all figured out for them.

"All right, boy, go inside and get washed up, or there won't be any chili left for you."

Foster charged through the door and disappeared inside the house to, hopefully, obey his father.

"Well, what do you say, El? You ready to be mine? Our son seems ready."

"Our son is also four. I'm not sure I trust his relationship expertise."

Jackson sat down next to her and pulled her into his lap. "I like the sound of that."

"Sound of what?"

"Our son."

"As long as you understand that when he misbehaves, he's your son." Eleanor settled back against his chest and pulled his arms around her waist. She tilted her head to the side and pushed her hair behind her ear and away from her neck. "Yes. I'm ready."

"You sure? You can't take it back, El. It's for always."

"I want always, Jackson." Eleanor covered his hands with hers and squeezed. "I love you."

"I'll always love you, El. But the mark will come later. Tonight. After we put our son to bed and have the rest of the night alone together." Jackson pressed his mouth to her neck and lightly bit down on her skin before releasing her with a gentle kiss. "Come on, let's get our son and grab dinner. I wasn't kidding about there not being any chili left."

TURN THE PAGE FOR *BROKEN SAGE* EXTRAS, INCLUDING

The official, Jules Crisare-Sanctioned "What Kind of Shifter are You?" Quiz

An excerpt from the next Broken Peak novel, *BROKEN MAGE*

And More!

THE OFFICIAL "WHAT KIND OF SHIFTER ARE YOU?" QUIZ

You've read *Broken Sage* and laughed at the pack's trick or treating exploits and cheered when Eleanor and Jackson found their happy ending. Right? I mean maybe you didn't do all those things, but let's just pretend you have. Now, I bet you're wondering where you'd fit in the pack. Would you be a wolf shifter? Or a griffin shifter? Or maybe another kind of shifter entirely. Well, you no longer have to wonder. In the short time it takes you to answer the questions below, you'll find out what kind of shifter you are.

WHAT SHIFTER AM I?

(If you want to find out what kind of shifter your partner is, replace "you" with "he/she/they". Depending on the result, you might want to keep it to yourself.)

1. When Vixen and Bray invite you to a barbecue at Broken Peak, you:

    a. hide in the woods and hope no one finds you

    b. show up earlier and be the last to leave and drink the most moonshine

2. Vixen asks you to steal a shifter artifact from a private collector who refuses to sell (there's no chance of getting caught), you:

    a. tell her no way

    b. tell her sure, why not

3. Vixen thinks you should find a mate, you:

    a. go out with whoever Mac recommends, and of course they're a perfect match, so you agree.

    b. create profiles on shifter-r-us with the rest of Broken Peak Pack and go out on group dates so your friends can give you instant advice. Plus, if they don't like your friends, they aren't for you.

4. War passed a new ordinance, barring all concealed weapons, even daggers, you:

a. don't bring the dagger Vixen got for you into town and leave it at home instead

b. ignore the ordinance, besides it's not like you go to War all that often

5. After a long day chasing down false alarms that led no where followed by a double dose of training from Vixen, you just want to go home and fall into bed, but your best friend sends a text, asking if you want to go out for dinner in thirty minutes, you:

a. call them back right away, since you plan on venting and your best friend is a great listener

b. ignore the message and call your friend back the next morning, you plan on spending the night alone with your favorite book

6. While walking through the park late at night with no one around, you see a new "Keep Off Grass" sign, you:

a. complain to yourself, but avoid walking on the grass

b. yank the sign out, throw it into the trees, then gleefully hop around on the grass since there's no more sign to stop you

ANSWERS

1. a=1, b=0

3. a=0, b=1

4. a=1, b=0

5. a=0, b=1

6. a=1, b=0

Add up your points! Have the number? Great, now if you scored:

0-1 GRIFFIN

Always up for a group hunt or hanging out with the pack, even if it means exploring forbidden territory.

2 WOLF

You take every opportunity to spend time with your friend and pack and always obey your Alpha.

3-4 COYOTE

You don't mind occasionally hanging out with friends, but prefer to spend most of your time alone with your still and never let something like rules get in the way of doing something.

5-6 BEAR

You're the strong and silent type, always ready to help your few close friends you have as long as your aren't breaking any rules.

AN EXCERPT FROM THE NEXT BROKEN PEAK PACK NOVEL, **BROKEN MAGE**

Leighton is a broken man with a broken wolf. Finding a mate is the last thing he needs or wants. But when a woman who risks her life to keep the shifters of Broken Peak Pack safe shows up in his territory, his wolf has other ideas. She's smart, funny, and sexy, but he's not worthy of a mate, especially a woman as good as Danielle.

"THEY'RE right behind me, aren't they?"

The general smiled, "I tried to warn you."

"No, you didn't. You said my last name in the same manner you've said it since you jumped in my car this morning, except this time you included a slight inflection at the end."

He released a long-suffering sigh and Danielle narrowed her eyes at him. If anyone should be sighing, she should be.

"Would you like to meet our hosts? Or would you prefer to keep your back to them and continue our conversation?"

"Neither." Danielle closed her eyes and wished she was anywhere but there. She didn't believe any of what she expressed about shifters being dangerous, but having nothing to base an analysis on, she pulled from the paranormal communities. The one point they all seemed to settle on was that skinwalkers were dangerous. Since the skinwalkers were the closest thing she found to shifters, she relied on the paranormal community for information, even if she didn't trust it.

Kernels of truth were located everywhere.

"I don't believe neither is an option, Ms. Howe."

"Well, until you add having the ground swallowing me whole, I'm sticking with neither."

A deep laugh rumbled from behind her, sending shivers along Danielle's spine.

"Looks like the ground is already doing a decent job of swallowing your shoes."

Danielle played through all her options, which included running away, and facing those she didn't want to face was nevertheless her best choice. Shit. A hundred times shit. Shit. Shit. Shit. Yeah, saying shit over and over in her mind wasn't helping. Time to pay the piper. Or face the piper, as the case may be.

Lifting one foot at a time, she pivoted on her toes to keep the ground from swallowing her shoes again, and almost turned right back around. One woman and two men stood in front of her. She recognized all three of them right away. There were few things in the world that lived up to anyone's expectations, the Grand Canyon being one, but Vixen somehow exceeded all of Danielle's expectations. The way she stood in the path, with a crooked smile and her palms on her hips, Vixen encompassed all the superheroes from the early days of comic books to the present flood of movies. Danielle figured the large, although large underplayed his sheer size, man standing beside Vixen with the smattering of gray in his hair was Bray, the man Vixen called mate. The third member of their welcoming party was the cowboy. Not that he was dressed as a cowboy now, but Danielle would have recognized his face in a sea of strangers.

Leighton.

Of all the members of Broken Peak Pack, he was the one she spent the most time fantasizing about in a totally not creepy way.

"For what it's worth, I don't believe anything I said. It's how I work. Gather all the data and give others the best of the information."

"The good news is you can go right to the source this time. The bad news is there's no one to give it to here, since everyone, well almost everyone, is a shifter and already possesses an intimate understanding of the subject matter." Vixen winked at her.

Actually winked. Danielle almost swooned at the gesture.

"We have a ways to go to get back to the Lodge, mind if we walk and talk?" Bray asked.

Danielle bobbed her head up and down. It was one thing to sit behind a desk in front of a bank of computer screens and peek into the lives of shifters, but standing in the presence of real live breathing shifters was something else altogether.

The General filed past Danielle and matched strides with Bray and Vixen further down the path.

Leighton leaned against a tree, crossed his arms over his massive chest, and tucked his hands under his armpits, while studying Danielle. The position of his arms lifted the bottom of his shirt, baring his defined stomach muscles. It didn't help matters that his worn jeans rode low on his hips. And it wasn't just the six pack, or maybe it was an eight pack. She didn't want him catching her staring at, but also the twin muscles that formed his Apollo's belt and pointed down.

Did shifters read minds?

She gulped and willed her mind to go blank. But then a hybrid version of the Stay-Puft Marshmallow man as the wolfman invaded her thoughts and lumbered around her brain.

Oh, God, this was bad. This was so bad.

Leighton combed his fingers through his light brown hair and shook his head from side-to-side. "You smell scared. You don't have to be scared of me. Of us."

Danielle let out a loud breath that was more huff than sigh. "I'm not scared."

He sniffed at the air. "Don't lie."

"Fine. You don't scare me." Danielle crossed her arms over her chest and stared at the ground between them.

Instead of erasing her investigation of the Pack like she should have, Danielle smuggled one of the files out of the Company. Leighton's file came home with her. When she couldn't sleep, she didn't listen to her podcasts. She read the few public records about him she managed to recover. Danielle memorized every broken bone, burn, and mark the doctors and nurses wrote down on his hospital records. And that his mother never brought him to the same hospital twice. Not to cover what appeared to be a history of abuse, but because they had a bigger secret to keep hidden. Then the records ceased. If Danielle didn't know any better, she would have guessed he died. Danielle had wanted to learn more about Leighton. But now that she was within arm's reach of him, she required a long shower to rinse away the film of shame from digging into his life.

Leighton didn't frighten her, that was the truth. The idea of him finding out she violated his privacy out of curiosity and would hate her for it scared the hell out of her.

She chanced lifting her head and meeting his intense stare. The power of his brilliant blue eyes was too much. His blue eyes turned silver and distant, and Danielle dropped her gaze.

"Come on, let's move." Leighton pushed off the tree and stuffed his hands deep in his pockets as he followed the others.

He didn't bother to stick around and see if she would follow. Of course, he wouldn't. Why would Leighton bother with a computer geek like her? Danielle needed to stop her daydreaming and concentrate on figuring out what happened next. She wasn't naive. She couldn't live with the pack for the rest of her life, so she had to spend what time she had here to establish a plan.

Danielle rushed after him, holding her arms out to the side so she wouldn't tip over. Stupid General. He could have offered her a chance to purchase a different pair of shoes. Something without a heel. "Um, Leighton?"

The star of her fantasies looked over his shoulder, but didn't stop, or even slow his pace. "What?"

Danielle needed to wave a wand and disappear what the shifters overheard. But since that was hopeless, she could at least make it better. "I just wanted to say, about what I said?"

"You sure you can walk and talk at the same time with those shoes?" He spun and walked backward along the trail.

Show off.

She halted, planted her hands on her hips, and stomped her foot. Any other location and the sequence of gestures would have performed flawlessly. In the middle of nowhere, off the beaten path — literally, and Danielle made an ass of herself flailing around like a fish out of water.

"So the answer's no." Leighton kept his hands in his pockets instead of coming to her aid. "Come on. At the rate you're moving, it'll be dark by the time we get back to the Lodge."

Danielle choked back a strangled curse, but Leighton had already swung back around and was striding away from her. He was nothing like the man she imagined. She had envisioned the shifters as sort of chauvinistic, but also chivalrous. However, Leighton hadn't helped her at all. He wasn't even willing to listen to an apology. Granted, she hadn't said she wanted to apologize, but he could have at least heard her out. Instead, he ridiculed and insulted her.

She did the only thing she could and stumbled after him, vowing that the first item she planned to acquire, once she decided where to go next, was a nice sturdy pair of boots.

Like the Grand Canyon, and unlike Leighton, the boots would live up to her expectations.

DATE NIGHT
A SILVER SENTINEL SHORT STORY

"I wanna have a kiki." Danielle flipped her newly dyed turquoise hair in a circle before posing like a vogue cover model and grinning at Finley.

"Lock the doors tight." Finley grinned back at Danielle and stomped his way up and down the hallway like he was walking the runway at Fashion Week.

"Let's have a kiki." Danielle responded and followed up her hair swinging with more exaggerated posing.

Foster ran in between Danielle and Finley and posed dramatically with his knees bent and his arms raised. "Mother fucker!"

"Finley!" El and Jackson yelled out from the kitchen. Even though neither of them had actually witnessed the performance, hearing their young son yell out the curse word with so much excitement could only mean that Finley was involved.

"What!?! Danielle was the one who had the video playing!"

Jackson stalked down the hallway and scooped up his son, supporting his bottom with the strength of his forearm. El's appreciative staring at the muscles in his arms didn't go unnoticed. Hell, if it meant El would stare at him with that hungry look, he'd spend hours lifting his son up and down over his head.

"We asked you guys for one thing tonight. One. Thing. Spend time with Foster tonight, so El and I could have a nice, quiet night alone." If El wasn't around, Jackson probably, okay, definitely, would have laughed his ass off at watching both Finley and Foster sing one of the campiest songs on the planet (a very close second to The Ding Dong Song but the first time El had seen Danielle playing that on her computer screen, El made it clear to the entire pack that Foster was never allowed to see that video until he was at least forty years old).

"Yeah, a nice quiet night alone." Finley waggled his eyebrows at his packmate while lewdly thrusting his hips back and forth in time to his words.

"Are you sure you're an adult?" El stalked down the hallway with her hands firmly planted on her hips. "I swear, sometimes I think Foster is more mature than you."

"It's why I'm his favorite uncle."

"I'm not sure the reason behind you being his favorite uncle is something you want to be proud of." Jackson glared and bit down hard on the side of his cheek to stop himself from laughing. Laughing would just make El mad, and all his begging and pleading for their special date night would go out the window.

While El was busy pursing her lips and narrowing her eyes at Finley, Danielle was doing her best to sneak away from the scene of the crime. Her attempt at an escape was almost successful. She would have gotten away with it if Foster hadn't spotted her.

"Aunt Dan Dan! Where are you going? I wanna do the kiki dance again. And I can only do it with you."

"Hey what about me?" Finley's jaw dropped and his eyes grew wider while he held his arms out to the side with his shoulders lifted tight against his ears. "Am I chopped liver?"

Foster giggled loudly. "Noooo. You're uncle Finley!"

El covered her face with her palms and growled. Jackson loved it when his mate growled. It was adorably cute and wouldn't even scare a squirrel, but it did send his heart racing and his blood pumping. "Danielle…"

"Okay, I get it, I do." Danielle held her hands up in an attempt to placate El and did her best to smile innocently. "But in all fairness, Eleanor, it's catchy as all get out. Plus, Foster sneaked into my office and I didn't realize he was there when I was playing it. And by that time, it was too late."

"New rule. Disney videos only when I'm not around to approve what he's watching." El dropped her hands, let her head fall back, and stared at the ceiling. "Can I trust you to keep everything Disney friendly for the night? Or do I need to call in Bray and Vixen to watch him?"

"Yep." Finley winked at Foster and reached for him. "Come on, pup, let's go play with Danielle's hamster."

Before Jackson could stop him, Foster leaped from Jackson into Finley's waiting arms and wrapped his arms tightly around Finley's neck. "Yes!"

Jackson took the opportunity to wrap his arm around his mate's neck and pull her tight against his side. "Come on, El, Vixen won't let anything too horrible happen and we already planned the night."

El allowed him to lead her way and down the hall to their room, but she looked over her shoulder and glare at her friend. "We're not done talking about this, Danielle."

"Woman, shh, you know how protective Leighton and his wolf are when it comes to Danielle. Let's just pretend our son isn't dancing to a song while singing out mother fucker. At least for the night. Tomorrow morning we can yell at Finley and you can lecture Danielle. I promise."

"I don't lecture."

"Okay, then talk. For a long time. Without any interruptions from others." Jackson swung her up into his arms and planted a kiss on her forehead while she squealed out a giggle. God, he loved it when his mate giggled. Especially when it came out of nowhere. While she hadn't said as much, he didn't think El had done much giggling since adopting Foster. Jackson loved the idea that he was the one who caused such unbridled joy in his mate. "Remember what you promised?"

El blushed from the tips of her ears down to her toes, or at least he assumed it was to her toes, from the brightness of red flush to her cheeks. "Yes. I remember."

"Good." Jackson stepped into their bedroom and kicked the door closed behind him. Shifting El around so one arm supported her, he reached behind him and locked the door. A closed door meant enter, or at least it did according to Foster, and the last thing he wanted or needed was his son interrupting their very adult date night. A night he had planned for an eternity if the impatience of his cock was anything to go by. Jackson dropped her on the bed, watching her body with a hungry gaze as it bounced on the soft mattress.

El scooted back across the mattress to the headboard and perched up on her elbows while looking up at Jackson expectantly.

Jackson grinned. God, his mate was beautiful. And amazing. And fucking adorable, too. But he told her all those things at least a hundred times a day and even though he didn't think she ever got tired of hearing them, now wasn't the time to say them again.

Or maybe it was.

"You're gorgeous, El, you know that?"

Her grin grew as she reached down and pressed her hands against her belly. "Are you still going to say that when I'm huge, unable to get out of chairs without assistance, and have uncontrollable gas?"

"Yep."

"How do you know for sure?"

"Because." Jackson flopped down on the bed and landed between her spread legs. He kissed her belly, just beneath her hands, and looked up the length of her chest at her. "I'm never going to stop saying it. Ever."

El giggled and wriggled beneath him.

Jackson groaned and kissed his way up her stomach, between her breasts to her lips. He swept the tip of his tongue across her bottom lip, tasting the sweetness of the fruit she'd eaten earlier. She parted her lips, granting his tongue entry, and of course he obliged. He wrapped his arm around her shoulder and his free hand slid down the side of her body to her leg, pulling her closer to him.

El lifted her head up, but Jackson slid his hand around her shoulder to the back of her head. He wanted his mate. He always wanted his mate. But tonight, he wanted her on his terms and she promised. He'd control the kiss, just like he'd control everything else.

"El." Pulling away with a deep breath, he sighed out her name.

She opened her eyes and gazed up at him with still parted lips. The tip of her tongue brushed across her up lip, and Jackson groaned. He leaned down and kissed her again. His hand skimmed over her hip to the waist of the tight jeans she'd worn that hugged her perfect ass to perfection. He loved these jeans. Almost as much as he loved her and their son.

Jackson made quick work of the button and zipper and even pulled the tops of her jeans down to her hips with one hand. His fingers brushed against the top of her panties before sliding further down, stroking over the silk.

Fuck. She was wet. He groaned into her mouth. They had the entire night and Jackson had planned on spending hours re-exploring her body, but screw that. He was going to fuck her and then he was going to spend hours re-exploring her body and then fuck her again.

El lifted her hips, pressing up against her fingers.

Jackson pulled her head back by her hair, separating them enough so he could kiss his way along her jaw to her ear.

This time it was El who groaned.

Jackson bit down on the cord of her neck just below her ear.

El released a tiny growl.

Or at least Jackson thought it was a groan.

So fucking cute. And so fucking nervous, too.

Probably because they hadn't had any kind of night alone together. Sure, they stole fifteen minutes here and there, but they hadn't actually spent an entire night all alone together since, well since the one night Jackson never want to spend much time remembering. The night the government tried to get to Foster by kidnapping El. It backfired. Horribly. But still didn't make him very happy.

El's body tensed, and her muscles flexed and fluttered.

"El?"

She jerked her head up and looked up at him with those big eyes of hers, all the while chewing happily on her bottom lip. Fuck. Both he and his wolf loved it when she did things like that.

El was his. His and his wolf's. And he wouldn't have it any other way.

"Baby, we can just watch a movie or something. How about we take a bath? I bet we can convince Vixen to wrangle everyone up and keep them away while we take over the bath." They'd all moved rooms so many different times to accommodate all the additions to the pack, but the Lodge still only had one bathtub.

They really needed to get to town and update some bathrooms. If the little raccoon shifter finally got brave enough to approach the pack, they'd have to do another round of rearranging, even if she only stayed for a short time.

"No. I'm sure." El purred as certainty pushed against the nerves, settling Jackson's wolf.

His mate was amazing. He didn't have to ask his wolf needed the answer to, but she answered it anyway. El reached out and pulled Jackson closer, folding and wrapping her arms and legs around him. He settled against her as though he belonged there. And he did. He didn't belong anywhere else. And neither did she.

Jackson's mouth found hers again. Without any thought or conscious direction. Yeah, he was impatient, but then who wouldn't be? He lashed at her lips until she finally parted her mouth. El's arms tightened around his neck as she whimpered. And not in the bad way, either. The whimper shot right to his cock. Not like it could get any harder, but it sure as hell tried.

She wanted more from Jackson and he was going to give it to her. He was going to give her everything she wanted and then everything he wanted. Jackson pulled her closer as he rolled to her his back, keeping her with him. He couldn't stop the groan as her body pressed tight against his.

Mine.

Both he and his wolf agreed.

She's mine. All mine.

Jackson gripped her hair and pulled her back from him. Yeah, he wanted her, but he needed a few extra minutes or he'd shoot his load like some teenager. El pouted, but it didn't change his opinion. Except the pout reminded him he wanted her lips on other parts of his body. But that would come a lot later.

He didn't waste any time rolling off the bed to his feet and yanked his shirt up over his head. "Come on, El, you too. Off. Off. We don't need any clothes right now."

She followed his suggestion, but didn't get off the bed. It was both good and bad. Good, because he didn't have to do any fancy maneuvering, but bad because her body bounced and flounced while she stripped off her jeans and shirt and effectively distracted Jackson. Instead of working on getting his clothes off, he was busy staring at her lace covered breasts. He needed to remember to add more of those bras to the shopping list. Lace bras did great things to her breasts. Amazing things.

"You're a few items of clothing behind, Jackson." El reached behind her, as if she was about to remove her bra, but hesitated. "You need to catch up before I continue."

Fuck catching up. Jackson would fuck her with her bra and panties on or off. He needed her that badly. He probably would have been able to fuck fully dressed, but it would require a bit too much work and patience. The former was easily remedied by convincing her to strip, the latter was more difficult to solve. And frankly, he didn't want to bother with trying to keep patient.

Counting. Whenever things got bad, Vixen said to count. So that's what Jackson did. He reached forty-five before he finally got everything back under control enough for him to remove the rest of his clothing. And El watched every movement with an appreciative stare.

Jackson's gaze met El's stare for a moment before she lowered her eyes.

Fuck, that was sexy.

His cock throbbed in anticipation.

"El, lie back on the bed." He pushed his jeans down and stepped out of them as he approached the bed.

Her legs parted and Jackson had a clear view of the slightly darker fabric in the gusset of her panties. Not that she could hide her arousal from him, but he loved seeing evidence of it, and the darker fabric hinted at just how wet she was.

As he stood at the end of the bed, staring down at her, Jackson pushed his shoulders back. Her eyes grew, if it was even possible, and she licked her lips with the tip of her tongue. Jackson knew she enjoyed looking at his body probably more than he enjoyed appreciating hers. He paused and let her stare while he decided where to start. Granted, it didn't take too long. Stolen moments now and again didn't allow for much and he'd missed the taste of her. Kneeling between her legs, he pressed her knees back, opening her further to his gaze.

Too bad she still had her panties on.

But the remedy required slipping them off, and it would take too much time. He could rip them off. He'd done it in the past, but El always yelled at Jackson for destroying her lingerie after the fact, even if she enjoyed it at the moment.

El swallowed, but said nothing.

Jackson lifted his gaze to her eyes and swept his finger along the inside of her leg, where the elastic of her panties pressed against her skin.

Another audible swallow from El.

He hooked his finger inside the elastic and pulled it aside, baring her to him.

Holy fuck. El was neatly trimmed. He was agnostic when it came to those things and honestly couldn't care what she did, but everything below her clit was bare with a small patch of hair just above.

This time it was Jackson who swallowed hard.

El's breath caught and her hands fisted the comforter on top of the bed.

Jackson didn't ask any questions, but El nodded. Entreating him not to stop. He didn't plan on stopping anytime soon, but he loved that she wanted him to continue.

"Stay just as you are, El. Don't move."

El nodded.

She didn't even finish half the gesture before Jackson dove in. His hands slid down to cup her ass, and he pulled her closer. Starting at the inside of her right knee, he kissed his way up the inside of her thigh with light touches as he neared his ultimate goal.

But it wasn't enough. While his lips covered the skin of her thighs, his fingers tickled over the bare lips of her pussy.

El moaned and her hips lifted closer to his fingers, but she didn't closer her legs. Jackson's mouth neared its destination and his fingers confirmed just how wet she was for him.

He was done teasing.

His mouth dropped over her clit, and he tickled her with just the tip of his tongue.

Her hips jerked up and Jackson nipped at her clit with just enough pressure to remind her of her promise to stay put, but not actually cause her any pain. El lowered her hips and Jackson rewarded her with sliding a finger between her wet folds. He switched between licking and sucking on her clit while stroking his finger in and out of her.

From the way El threw her head from side to side and pulled at the comforter, she was struggling not to move.

Jackson slid a second then third finger into her. He allowed his tongue to delve lower and sweep into her along with his fingers. Not so much for her pleasure, but because he wanted to fully taste her.

"Jackson... please..." she dragged the s out into a soft whimper.

Jackson laughed out a slow breath. He had no idea whether she wanted more from him or release, but he wasn't going to ask. He pulled his fingers free from her pussy and replaced them with his tongue.

The volume of her whimpers increased until they turned into loud moans, which evolved into nonsensical cries.

This was as much for Jackson as El, and now that he had her undivided attention for over fifteen minutes, he didn't plan on stopping anytime soon. He took what he needed, enjoying the scent of her arousal with each breath he took and the sweet taste of her juices.

"Jackson... Please..." El hadn't given up on the pleading, but Jackson wasn't close to finishing with what he started.

"Jackson. I'm close. So close. Please." Her moans turned back into the whimpering and Jackson took pity on her.

It wouldn't be the last time they had a date night, and he'd be able to return to what had always been his favorite place to visit on El's body. His mouth returned to her clit, and he slid three fingers into her pussy. Working both her clit and her pussy at the same time, he curled his fingers up, brushing against the spot he knew would send her over the edge. She shattered, her body writhing beneath his and her pussy clamping down hard on his fingers. Jackson didn't stop. He doubled her efforts, pushing her over the edge again.

He almost joined her. The sounds coming from her mouth and the feel and taste of her nearly sent him over the edge too, but he pulled back. He could wait.

He brushed his fingers against that spot again, wanting to pull a third orgasm from her, and redoubled his efforts on her clit. Her body shuddered, and she screamed out in pleasure.

Fuck, she was beautiful when she came.

Jackson stopped, distracted by the sight of the orgasm rolling through her. If he didn't know better, he'd think this was her first orgasm. Once her body settled down and breathing evened out slightly, Jackson returned to her pussy, lapping up her wetness. Once she's clean enough for his satisfaction, he slid up her body and stretched out alongside her.

He pulled her close, cradling her body against his and stroking her back with light tickles, helping her ease through the aftershocks.

El looked up at him, and Jackson's mouth found hers. His hand cupped the back of her head and he pulled her closer to him so his tongue had an easier time of delving into her lush mouth.

When they finally parted, El grinned up at him. "Your turn?"

Jackson grinned and kissed her nose. "We can stay here together for a few minutes."

A beautiful naked woman laid in his bed and wouldn't be going anywhere anytime soon. Jackson had all the time in the world. He'd wait and savor the moment he had now. They had hours to go before morning.

Hours and hours to go.

ACKNOWLEDGMENTS

Sitting down to write an acknowledgment page is much like making an acceptance speech at an award's show. It's more than likely that you will forget someone and then have to spend hours on the phone apologizing for the misstep. And God help you, if it's your mother. So, I should probably get that one out of the way first, right? I need to acknowledge my parents, especially my mother, who have supported me and define the phrase unconditional love.

The readers of the Broken Peak Pack and the Sentinels of the Silver Orb. Without them, there would be no Vixen and Bray.

Much gratitude and thanks to Chantel. She's an unconditional pillar of support and encouragement. Everyone needs a Chan in their life.

I would be remiss in not thanking my friends and family, who put up with me during my seclusion in the writing cave and constantly offer their support and love.

Finally, and of course not least, the wonderful individuals who are responsible for the creation of the collector's edition of the Broken Peak Pack Omnibus: Kasey S., Sherry M., Meg M., Pyndan, Erin C., Rhel, Kieran, Rafael P, Sarah, and Melanie B. Little did they know that by supporting one little Kickstarter, they'd find a permanent spot on my acknowledgments page.

ACKNOWLEDGMENTS

[illegible]

ABOUT THE AUTHOR

Jules Crisare loves writing sexy shifter romances. The growly and dominant males of Broken Peak and the Silver Sentinels are the ones bending to the strong wills of the smart heroines who cross their paths. Seriously, only strong heroines need apply to capture the hearts of these sexy alphas. Get your shifter loving fingers ready to turn those pages and explore the world of the Sentinels of the Silver Orb.

www.JCrisare.com

www.ingramcontent.com/pod-product-compliance
Lightning Source LLC
Chambersburg PA
CBHW031232210726
48287CB00003B/750